CW00665854

ONE LAST SUMMER AT SEABREEZE FARM

JO BARTLETT

Boldwood

First published in 2020. This edition first published in Great Britain in 2023 by Boldwood Books Ltd.

Copyright © Jo Bartlett, 2020

Cover Design by Debbie Clement Design

Cover photography: Shutterstock

The moral right of Jo Bartlett to be identified as the author of this work has been asserted in accordance with the Copyright, Designs and Patents Act 1988.

All rights reserved. No part of this book may be reproduced in any form or by any electronic or mechanical means, including information storage and retrieval systems, without written permission from the author, except for the use of brief quotations in a book review.

This book is a work of fiction and, except in the case of historical fact, any resemblance to actual persons, living or dead, is purely coincidental.

Every effort has been made to obtain the necessary permissions with reference to copyright material, both illustrative and quoted. We apologise for any omissions in this respect and will be pleased to make the appropriate acknowledgements in any future edition.

A CIP catalogue record for this book is available from the British Library.

Paperback ISBN 978-1-80162-044-4

Large Print ISBN 978-1-80162-045-1

Harback ISBN 978-1-80162-043-7

Ebook ISBN 978-1-80162-046-8

Kindle ISBN 978-1-80162-047-5

Audio CD ISBN 978-1-80162-038-3

MP3 CD ISBN 978-1-80162-039-0

Digital audio download ISBN 978-1-80162-041-3

Boldwood Books Ltd
23 Bowerdean Street
London SW6 3TN
www.boldwoodbooks.com

For my inspirational cousin, Kathy, who's shown us all what living the best life you can really means xx

1

'How long have I got?' Georgia locked eyes with her consultant, who ran a finger around the inside of his shirt collar before clearing his throat. She could see him breathing in and out, and she concentrated on copying the rhythm because she seemed to have forgotten how to do it automatically. The rest of her life hung on his answer. No wonder she'd forgotten how to breathe.

'I can't predict that, but if there are things you want to do... I wouldn't put them off.'

'There must be something you can do!' Gabe got to his feet, with Georgia's mother just behind him. It was always going to be a race to see which of them would demand a miracle first. They wanted Georgia to recover, but it was time to stop pretending. She was grateful for the doctor's honesty. If time was limited, she didn't want to spend it thinking about dying. She needed to live. The terror that crept in when she was on her own needed to be kept at bay at any cost.

'I'm really sorry, but we're running out of options. The years that Georgia has been having dialysis have started to affect her, and the symptoms she's been experiencing lately are because her heart is in danger of failing. If she can't get a transplant soon she'll be too poorly to receive one, because her heart won't be able to take the strain. I really wish there was something else we could do.'

'What about a kidney transplant, so she can come off dialysis for a bit?' Georgia's mother, Caroline, sat back down with a thud. 'If things are this bad, surely we can think again about me donating a kidney to tide her over?'

'Sadly it's not an option.' Mr Kennedy was nothing if not patient and he'd probably explained this to Caroline a hundred times over the last few years. 'There's some evidence that coming off dialysis could reduce the risk of Georgia's heart failing, but her diabetes would be likely to damage the transplanted kidney unless she gets a new pancreas too, which obviously rules out live donation. And, sadly, with Georgia's blood type and increased antibodies, finding a matching double donor in time is a long shot. That's why she's been on the transplant list for so long.'

'But if a new kidney lets her come off dialysis for a bit and buys her a bit more time, while she waits for a pancreas, it's got to be worth it?' Caroline looked at Gabe, who nodded, but the consultant was already shaking his head.

'We'd never get ethics approval to transplant a kidney just to bridge the gap when we know that won't last. Especially with so many other candidates on the list who haven't got as many complications as Georgia. Even if that wasn't an issue, we've already ruled you out as a live donor.'

'I'm dieting like mad. If I can reverse the Type 2 diabetes, then surely the option is back on the table?' Caroline's eyes filled with tears. 'I can't believe that's what's standing in the way of me helping my own daughter.'

'Can everyone please stop talking about me as if I'm not

here?' Georgia clenched her fists. They were wasting time and she didn't have that luxury any more. She'd been diagnosed with Type 1 diabetes at the age of seven and by twenty-two she'd had to go on dialysis. Complications of the diabetes had led to anaemia and eventually a blood transfusion, which had resulted in her body making more antibodies than it should. All of which made it much more difficult to find a match for a transplant.

The stress of her illness had taken its toll on her mother over the years as well. Too many late nights at the hospital, focusing on making Georgia's diet as healthy as possible instead of taking care of herself, had led to her mother neglecting her own health a long time ago. The diagnosis of Type 2 diabetes had still come as a shock to both of them though, and Caroline had been wracked with guilt because it ruled her out of ever being a live donor. Not that Georgia would have let her mother donate her kidney anyway, even if the doctors had agreed. It wasn't worth the risk to Caroline, when it would only buy her two or three years off dialysis at best. They'd all chased the holy grail of 'when you get better' for far too long. It was time to stop waiting and start living; not just for Georgia, but for her mother as well.

'I know you can't predict exactly, Mr Kennedy, but how long would you guess I've got if your life depended on it? Because mine kind of does.' Georgia had a habit of making jokes when everyone around her was in tears. Sometimes it upset her mum, but the alternative was to admit how awful things were and, if she did that, there was a danger she might forget how to laugh altogether.

'I'd say around a year.' Mr Kennedy shuffled some papers. Things were really serious when even her consultant couldn't look Georgia in the eyes and the creeping terror was trying to make its way up her spine. She had to start making plans and fill her days, to leave as little space as possible for the terror to find a gap. It was now or never.

'In that case, I'd better get on with doing the things I want to, like you said.' She stood up and held out her hand to the consultant, hoping that none of them could tell she was shaking. 'Thank you for always being upfront with me. You promised me that's what you'd do when I first met you and you've never let me down.'

'We'll do whatever we can to give you the best quality of life for as long as possible.' Mr Kennedy gave her a half-smile and Georgia mirrored the action. Quality of life was the best she could hope for now – the best anyone could when it came down to it – and she wasn't going to waste another second.

* * *

'Where's your mum?' Gabe stood by the kettle as he waited for it to boil and anyone casually observing them would probably have assumed it was his house. He was as much a part of the furniture as the huge Welsh dresser that took up the whole of one wall, which the previous occupants had decided was too big for them to try and move. Gabe had been Georgia's constant companion since they'd first come into each other's lives at a mother and baby group, and she couldn't remember a significant event since then that hadn't involved him.

'She's taken Barney for a walk. She always does that when she needs a bit of time to think, or to scream with frustration.' Georgia had her back to Gabe, as she took the cake tin out of the cupboard. Some things were easier to say when she wasn't looking into his eyes.

'Maybe I should have gone with her.' His voice sounded

strained. 'Screaming might not help, but it makes a lot more sense than standing here making tea, when the whole world's falling apart.'

'Not the whole world, Gabe, just my body. And we both knew that would happen sooner or later.' Georgia hoped to God that he wasn't going to lose his sense of humour when she needed it more than ever. She was counting on him. Having Gabe was the main reason she'd been able to keep laughing, when part of her wanted to be out there with her mum, screaming in frustration too. But that wouldn't have helped any of them.

'I'm not ready, George.' He looked across and it was obvious he was trying not to cry, but if he did they both knew she'd give him hell. What he didn't know was that it was a diversion from her own emotions; she'd never cried in front of him and she wasn't about to start now. Thank God he didn't let her down. 'I was hoping you'd at least have the chance to get a bit saggy on the outside, before your body gave up on the inside.'

'That's more like it.' She laughed, the tension lifting as she took the lemon cake out of the tin. It was a diabetes and dialysis-friendly recipe that her mother had perfected over the years, but it tasted surprisingly good. Even if it was just about the only sweet treat she seemed to be allowed these days. 'According to Mr Kennedy, I've got a year left to get saggy and to do everything else I've ever wanted to do. I'm not going to be able to fit it all in, but I'll do my best.'

'What have you got in mind?' Gabe was scanning her face as she turned to look at him.

'Put it this way, Mum's not going to like any of it, but time's running out.' Georgia knew she sounded matter of fact, but she needed to be practical. There was no time to wallow even if she'd wanted to. The fact that she wouldn't be getting the average eighty years on earth was out of her control. But any regrets she had about wasting the time she had left would be on her. 'For as long as I can remember, all I've ever been told is "you can do that when you get better", but I'm not going to get better, am I?'

'There's still a chance.'

'Gabe, don't, *please*. I need you to be on my side.' Reaching out, she squeezed his hand; her oldest friend, her ally through everything and the one person who'd never treated her as if she was different. They couldn't hide behind platitudes now. 'Okay, I'm dying, but that makes it more important than ever that I live every single second I've got left. I'm not going to wait around for a miracle.'

'I can understand that.' Gabe nodded several times, as if he was trying to shake off the instinct he'd always had to protect her. 'So what's on your bucket list?'

'Well, for a start it's not a bucket list – everyone has those and you know I like to be special.' She grinned. 'Mine is a to-do list. and if you even think about setting up a Go Fund Me page in my name, I will never, ever, speak to you again!'

'Okay, scout's honour.' He held up three fingers in a mock salute. His laugh was one of her favourite sounds in the world and one of the things she was going to miss the most. 'What's on this not-a-bucket list then?'

'Loads of little things, but there's a big top three that I'll be really annoyed about if I don't do them by the time I shuffle off.'

'I don't want you haunting me, so I suppose we'd better get them sorted.' Gabe pulled a face, defaulting to the same coping mechanism Georgia used: laughing at something that would otherwise be a nightmare. 'Come on then, hit me with your top three.'

'Number one, I want to spend the summer living by the

sea.' Georgia turned and opened the blind on the kitchen window, revealing the street outside. The same street that she and Gabe had grown up on, a few doors apart. The front door of the house she shared with her mother opened straight on to the pavement and there were people hurrying past the window. If she left the blind open, it wouldn't be long before someone stopped and stared in. Before she died she wanted to live somewhere that had a direct view of the sea and no need for blinds. If she couldn't afford that, then a sea view within strolling distance – which was all she could do these days – would have to do.

'Right, that sounds relatively straightforward.' Gabe poured out some tea, passing Georgia the half-sized cup she always used because of the restrictions dialysis had made to her fluid intake. 'What else is on the list?'

'I want to raise some money for charity, but not through some Go Fund Me or Just Giving donations.' Georgia narrowed her eyes, daring him to object. 'I want to raise the money myself with something art related if I can, and I want the money to go towards helping other people who want to achieve things they might not be able to otherwise. Or maybe towards buying things that can go into hospitals and treatment centres to help relieve the sheer, unrelenting boredom of regular visits.'

'More challenging, but still doable, and maybe that's something I could help with.' Gabe sounded relieved. They'd followed each other to primary and secondary school, then on to art school and, finally, university. If he hadn't been such a talented photographer, she'd have wondered if he'd gone to the same art college and university just to keep an eye or her, at the request of her mother. But he couldn't fake his passion for photography.

'You could definitely help with that.' She hesitated, almost certain she was about to whip Gabe's sense of relief away from him with what she said next. 'Which takes us on to item number three on the list.'

'Is that something else I can help with?' Gabe would do anything for her, but this might be too much, even for him.

'I want a baby.' Georgia had to press her lips together to stop herself from laughing at the look on his face. His mouth was moving, but for a good few seconds nothing came out. Finally he managed to speak.

'George, I don't think a baby's a good idea. Could your body even get through a pregnancy?'

'I'm not sure it can even get through the day.' She was going to have to put him out of his misery. 'So I'll settle for a puppy, but I need to know for certain that he or she has a home for life when I'm gone, and Barney's too old to cope with having a puppy running rings around him.'

'I'll take the dog, if it comes to that.' Gabe put an arm around her shoulders and for a moment she left herself relax against his chest; she was going to miss this so much too. 'But I still think something's going to change, George. You're not going anywhere yet, but I want to do everything I can to help you cross those things off your list anyway.'

'Thank you.' Resting her head on his shoulder, she sighed. If she wasn't careful, she could convince herself he was right, but her days had been numbered for a long time and now the countdown had sped up. Gabe had always been there, protecting her from insensitive comments from other kids, through to downright bullying, for more than twenty years since her initial diagnosis. But even he couldn't fix things this time.

2

Caroline sat at the kitchen table scrolling through her messages for the third time, and then flicked back to Richard's profile.

'What do you think, Barney? Should I agree to meet him?' She'd been corresponding with Richard for the last two weeks and he seemed very nice, but the truth was she'd only ever agreed to sign up to the dating website in the first place to please Georgia. Caroline nudged Barney, who was steadfastly ignoring her question in favour of snoring at a volume a Boeing 747 would be proud of. She'd cried into the old Boxer dog's fur more times than she could remember, mostly over Georgia, and he'd never once tired of comforting her. But when it came to matters of the heart, it turned out Barney had little to no interest in offering advice.

'Have you arranged to meet him yet? Just do it!' Georgia suddenly appeared behind her, making her jump. She'd known it wasn't Barney – obviously if he did ever elect to speak, his voice would be several octaves lower – but getting an answer to her question was still a surprise, and she couldn't think of a single excuse not to reply to Richard's latest message that Georgia would swallow.

'He wants to meet me for a drink tomorrow, at the Silver Seagull in Kelsea Bay.'

'Ooh fancy!' Georgia gave a little sway of her hips before breaking out into the broad grin that had always been her trademark. 'How many excuses have you come up with so far?'

'About twenty-five, but he's found a way around all of them.' Caroline wrinkled her nose.

'He sounds like a keeper already, let me take another look at his profile.' Gently elbowing her out of the way, Georgia grabbed the laptop. 'He looks lovely. Perfect stepdad material and he seems to like all the same things you do, plus he's got a Fitbit on in one of his pictures, so you'll be able to step your way to victory together.'

'I've lost twenty-two pounds so far, so it's definitely working. I know I hated the bloody thing nagging me to get up every hour at first, but the diabetes nurse at the GP's surgery said I should have completely reversed my symptoms by the end of the year.'

Since being diagnosed with Type 2 diabetes, Caroline had thrown herself headlong into an exercise and healthy eating plan. She did 10,000 steps, every day, even if that meant doing fifty-seven laps around the kitchen last thing at night until the damn thing finally buzzed to tell her she'd hit her target. She was on the five-two diet as well, and mostly sticking to healthy options, even on the unrestricted days, but everyone deserved a treat now and then. She was only human after all.

'You've done brilliantly, Mum.' Georgia sat down next to her on the sofa and there wasn't a trace of bitterness in her voice. It always amazed her how her daughter seemed to take her illness in her stride. Caroline had a feeling that Georgia wasn't nearly as stoic as she made out, but her humour and bravado was a disguise she never took off. At least not in front of anyone. The least Caroline could do was try to be half as brave and to stop taking the good health she'd been gifted for granted.

Georgia had never had the option of dieting and exercising herself back to health. The type of diabetes her darling girl suffered from had no known cause, it was just the worst kind of luck, and the difficulties the medical team had experienced in getting her insulin levels right when she was a teenager had started the kidney damage that was now in its final stage.

The doctors couldn't say whether the failure of Georgia's kidneys was down to the diabetes alone, but they didn't think so, as they'd all worked hard to follow the doctor's advice. It was possible that she'd been born with kidneys that weren't working the way they should and the diabetes had just finished the job. Those consultations broke Caroline's heart and she'd felt like punching the wall more than once at the unfairness of it all. Wasn't it enough that Georgia's father had been killed in an accident, before she'd even had a chance to make memories with him, and that they'd had to cope with her illness without his support?

Caroline had bought Basil, their first Boxer, three months after losing Georgia's dad, Mark. Georgia had been four at the time and they hadn't discovered her diabetes until three years later. Basil had lived until Georgia was fifteen and neither of them could face getting another dog. Then, when Georgia and Gabe had headed off to university at eighteen, the house had been too quiet for Caroline to stand it any more and she'd decided to get Barney. He was ten now, and could only manage to accompany her for about a thousand of the steps she did every day, but she couldn't imagine life without him. Now the doctors were asking her to imagine a life without Georgia too and that was something she couldn't even try to do. She wouldn't.

Researchers were coming up with new treatments all the time and if anyone deserved a bit of luck it was Georgia. Caroline hadn't given up on persuading the doctors to change their minds about a transplant either. She'd lobby the ethics committee and chain herself to the building where they met if she had to. If they'd have let her, she'd have given up her pancreas and her life for her daughter. With Georgia having so many antibodies, as a result of a blood transfusion when she was younger, just finding a compatible blood group wasn't enough. She needed a tissue match too, to give the transplant a good chance of working. So the chance of finding a stranger on the donor register who was a match, before Georgia's heart was too weak, was almost nil, and only a few centres of excellence offered pancreatic transplants anyway. It was several months until the transplant laws would be changing and people would have to opt out if they didn't want to donate organs after their death, but that could make all the difference. Georgia just had to hold on and defy the doctors' predictions, like she'd been doing since the day she was born.

'There's another upside to all that weight loss you know.' Georgia wiggled her eyebrows. 'Now that you're looking so fantastic, it's time to make good on your promise of going on *at least* three dates with someone from the dating site, and Richard looks as good a bet as any of them to me.'

'It's all right you saying I've got to have three dates with him, but what if he runs for the hills after one?' Caroline squinted at Richard's picture again. She had to admit, he did have a kind face.

'He won't, but if he does, he's an idiot. You can just start over again, until you find one that you can have three dates with. I know what you'll do otherwise, talk yourself out of seeing him again after the first date, just like you've done with all the others.'

'You make it sound like there's been loads of them!' Caroline laughed and Georgia rested her head against her mother's.

'Not loads, but I'd like there to be at least one who could be in with the chance of becoming someone special. It's been nearly twenty-five years since Dad died and I don't want you to be on your own when I'm gone.'

'You're not going anywhere.'

'Mum!' Georgia's tone was sharp as she jolted her head away, and Caroline bit her lip.

'All right, let's not get into another argument about it. I've promised to do the tasks you've got on your list for me by the end of the summer and I will.' After the consultant had told Georgia in January that she might only have a year to live, it was as if someone had lit a fire underneath her. She'd set herself three big goals, as she put them, and made a list of lots of other little things she wanted to see happen. If it distracted Georgia from thinking about how quickly the weeks were flying past, then it had to be a good thing. Caroline couldn't stop herself thinking about it though and no number of distractions were going to change that. She'd had to throw out the wooden calendar that had always sat on the windowsill, where blocks were turned over to mark each new day and passing month. Turning them over every morning had felt so wrong. She wanted time to stand still, so she could keep Georgia forever. As much as Caroline had always loved the changing seasons – each of them bringing special occasions to share with her daughter – if the upcoming summer never ended, it would be fine by her.

* * *

Georgia looked from the computer screen to the wheelchair and back again. There was no getting away from the fact that it represented the next stage of her illness but, worse than that, it was ugly. Black, grey and boring, with *Property of Elverham Hospital* stamped on the back. She wasn't at the stage where she needed to use a wheelchair yet, but if she was going to end up needing it to get out and about as much as she could, then it was going to get a makeover.

'Look, I've found a Pinterest site called Pimp Your Chair and there's one here that's got beads on the spokes exactly like I had on my bike in Year Six.' Georgia turned the screen towards Gabe and he laughed.

'I remember that bike. You were the only one who had to take your cycling proficiency test three times because you fell off every time you turned a corner!'

'I had dyspraxia.' Georgia couldn't help laughing too, as Gabe raised his eyebrows. 'All right, self-diagnosed and some might say I was just hopelessly clumsy.'

'Cute, though. Do you remember that phase you went through where you wouldn't go anywhere without wearing your *Busted* T-shirt? You even had it on under your school uniform on our last day of primary school.'

'I thought I was so cool back then. No wonder you had to save me from getting beaten up so often when we started secondary school. All the other kids were into Linkin Park and The White Stripes, or at least they pretended to be.' She grinned again. 'But we all know who your favourite was!'

'They weren't my favourite, I just always thought their songs had brilliant melodies. And I don't care what anyone says, I still like Westlife.'

'No-one could ever accuse you of being cool, Gabe, and that's just one of the many reasons why I love you!' She'd been sixteen the first time she'd told Gabe she loved him, when he'd spent an hour travelling back to the bus station after they'd got home from school and she'd realised she'd left her GCSE art folder on the bus. She'd already felt close to a hypo and her low blood sugar level readings had backed that up, so there was no chance of her being able to travel to see if the folder had been handed in. When Gabe finally got back – holding the folder in his arms – telling him she loved him had been the only appropriate response. He was the best friend anyone could ask for.

'It didn't stop you spreading the rumour that I cried when Brian McFadden left the group.' Gabe gave her a playful nudge, always judging it just right so that he didn't make her feel like she was made of glass, but never risking hurting her either.

'Look me in the eye and tell me you didn't cry!'

'I just thought he was throwing it all away, that's all.' Gabe's forehead creased as he frowned. 'But you telling everyone set the seal on my reputation for the whole of secondary school.'

'I'm sorry.' She linked her arm through his, knowing he'd long since forgiven her. 'But I had to take the heat off myself, after Sally Barrymore told everyone that they could catch diabetes from me if I touched them.'

'She was horrible and you did me a favour anyway. All the other boys thought I was good, old, harmless Gabe, whose love of Westlife must mean I was no threat to them when it came to girls. It worked a treat and I got off with at least five girls over our shared love of Shane Filan.'

'How did I never know that!' She widened her eyes. She'd have bet her last pound that she knew everything about Gabe, but sometimes he still had the capacity to surprise her. Although it wasn't really a shock to discover he was such as hit with the girls they'd been at school with. He had always been tall, even in year seven, with laughing green eyes and slightly wavy hair that never did what he wanted it to, but somehow suited him perfectly. There were times over the years when she'd wondered if their friendship would have developed into something else, if he hadn't always had to play the role of her protector, but overall she was glad it hadn't. She'd rather have him as a friend forever – her version of it anyway – than have had to watch him move on to the next Westlife fan that caught his attention. The fact that somewhere along the line she'd fallen in love with him, was the one secret she'd never shared and the one thing she'd never tell him, not even now.

It had happened gradually, maybe that GCSE art folder had been the start – she couldn't be sure. But telling him she loved him over the years had become such a simple truth, like saying the sky was blue. There was never a big revelation because it had always been out there. Except she'd didn't just love him, she was *in love* with him, and there was a huge difference. Holding her feelings in was how Georgia had survived and it was no different when it came to Gabe. The risk of letting how she really felt about dying out in to the open was that those feelings might completely overwhelm her. Laying how she felt about Gabe on the line and being rejected, however gently, would kill her long before she took her last breath and she needed him by her side right to the end.

'You didn't know because you didn't think of me that way. I mean neither of us ever saw each other that way, did we? We were more like brother and sister.' Gabe shrugged, blissfully unaware of the thoughts that were running through her head. 'So are we ordering some of these beads for the spokes? I thought maybe some tinsel streamers for the handle bars and a Barbie bicycle horn?'

'I'll do it if you get yourself a *Power Rangers* BMX again like you had in primary school and ride alongside me.'

'I think my mum still has it in the shed, but I'd be like one of those clowns riding a tricycle.'

'Even better!' Georgia laughed. 'That'll be another one of my goals crossed off the not-a-bucket list, taking every last chance to take the mickey out of you. But I still have the biggest thing to sort out and I've got no idea where to start.'

'Have you narrowed it down to where you want to live?' Gabe had never once told her that the idea was crazy and she should just forget about living by the sea and stay at home with her mum, where she'd be safe. Her mother hadn't been able to stop herself, though, which meant she was all the more grateful for his support.

'I need to be less than half an hour from the hospital, forty-five minutes at a push.'

'In that case, give me a minute and we'll get this narrowed down to a location at least.' Gabe jumped off the sofa and went to the front door. Ten seconds later she heard the car door slam and he was back on the sofa within the promised minute.

'An atlas?' Her eyebrows shot up behind her fringe as he put the book down next to her. 'Who the hell still has an atlas? Remind me to buy you a sat nav for Christmas, if I'm still around by then.'

'George, don't... I'm okay with all of this, taking the mickey out of each other like we always have and making light of what's going on, but I can't think about you not being here. I can't picture it and I don't want to. Not until I have to.'

'Okay, let's go back to me laughing at you for still having an atlas then.' The backs of Georgia's eyes were burning, but she blinked hard. Over the years she'd come to terms with the prospect of dying, but it was the thought of hurting Gabe and her mum that always hit Georgia hardest. She was going to miss them both like crazy; they were her entire world, but hopefully she'd have no awareness of it. They would, though, and they'd have to carry on without her. At least they had each other, but she wanted more than that for both of them. Even if she couldn't bear the thought of Gabe finding someone else whilst she was still around, however selfish that might be.

'You'll be envying my atlas in a minute!' Gabe flicked the book open to the page with Elverham on it, the town where Georgia's dialysis unit was located. 'All we need to do is use the key to measure a fifteen mile radius from the hospital.'

'Now you're using an atlas key? Do I even know you?'

Ignoring her, Gabe marked out a rough circle, containing all the places that were fifteen miles or fewer from the hospital, at least a third of the circle sweeping along the Kent coast. 'See anywhere you fancy?'

'I'd be happy with anywhere on the coast, if I could find somewhere at the right price.'

'What about if money was no object? Where would you pick then?'

'Kelsea Bay, obviously.' Georgia ran a finger over the words that spelled out the seaside village that had always been her happy place. 'But there's no way I could afford to live there and, before you even suggest it, I am never going to reconsider the idea of having a Go Fund Me page. There are far more important causes people could be donating to.'

'People would want to do it for you, George.'

'I don't want everyone knowing how ill I am, or how little time I might have left. Every time I've had something new diagnosed, people start to look at me in a different way and I don't want to spend my last year with a crick in my neck, whilst I try to make eye contact with people who've got their heads tilted to one side in that classic *poor-little-Georgia* way.' Sympathy had always been her kryptonite, because she was never closer to tears than when other people were overcome with emotion. But she wanted to go out the way she'd always lived, keeping her deepest fears to herself.

'Fair enough, but I think we should go to Kelsea Bay and have a look around anyway. You never know, there might be something you can stretch to within your budget. I'm down there on Friday to photograph a One Wish wedding.'

'Another one?' Gabe was never going to make the sort of money he deserved to, when he seemed to spend half his life giving away his work for free, but she understood why he did it and he wouldn't be Gabe without his great, big, generous heart. One Wish was a charity that made dreams come true for people who were living with life-limiting conditions, or who were terminally ill. They arranged everything from weddings to children meeting their favourite celebrities, and almost all the families involved wanted those precious moments captured on film forever. That was where Gabe came in and the resulting photographs were always breath-taking. As far as Georgia knew, Gabe hadn't once turned down a request for his help and that was just one more reason why she loved him.

'It's at Seabreeze Farm.'

'I'm in. You had me at Kelsea Bay, but Seabreeze Farm is an offer you know I'll never turn down.' Although the farm was mostly a wedding venue now, when Georgia had been growing up, it had operated as a donkey sanctuary and it had been her favourite place in the whole world. There was a fabulous tearoom up there too and it was somewhere she'd often headed to escape when things got too much. It was where she'd gone when she'd finally had to admit she needed to give up working as an art therapist, at the same hospital where she received her dialysis treatment. She'd ended up missing too many days due to sickness, as her condition continued to deteriorate, and she'd hated letting people down. Allowing someone more reliable to take over seemed the right thing to do, even if it had been one of the hardest things to accept.

'Friday at Seabreeze Farm is a date then.' Gabe caught her eye for a second and something fluttered in her chest that had nothing to do with her failing heart.

3

_____

Ellie pinched the skin between her thumb and the first finger of
her left hand, in a vain attempt to hold back the threatened
tears. Ever since they'd agreed to host a One Wish wedding at
Seabreeze Farm, she'd been trying her hardest to hold in her
emotions when she was around the couple getting married and
their families. One Wish was organising the wedding in a very
short period of time. The bride-to-be, Rose, who had motor
neurone disease and whose health was deteriorating scarily
quickly, had spent all of her childhood holidays in Kelsea Bay.
Rose and her fiancé, Dave, were both in their late sixties and
they'd been living together for more than twenty years, as
second time around'ers, after their first marriages hadn't
worked out. Rose had told Ellie that they'd never seen a reason
to get married, until her diagnosis, and now it was the one
thing she wanted more than anything, whilst she could still
walk down the aisle.

When Ellie and her mother, Karen, had inherited the farm
– an ex-donkey sanctuary – from her great-aunt Hilary, turning
it into a wedding venue had been a way of paying for the

upkeep of the animals and the almost constant maintenance on the farm, which was perched high on the cliffs overlooking the English Channel. In the five years since they'd taken over the farm, they'd expanded to offer honeymoon and holiday accommodation, after converting some outbuildings. Things had changed for them on a personal front too, with her mother marrying Alan, the farmer who owned the property next door, and Ellie marrying the local vet, Ben. The arrival of their daughter, Mae, the Christmas before last, and Alan's reunion with Freya, the daughter he hadn't even known he had, meant there hadn't been a dull moment since they'd arrived in Kelsea Bay.

The weddings and parties they hosted regularly reminded Ellie that she had the best job in the world, even when she was up at five in the morning feeding the donkeys and other animals that were a hangover from the farm's days as a sanctuary. She was clearly cut from the same cloth as her great-aunt, as she'd added to the menagerie over the years with animals who might have been put down otherwise. But nothing had ever felt more rewarding than hosting Rose and Dave's wedding. When Ellie had spotted a post from One Wish on a Kelsea Bay community page on Facebook, looking for suppliers to donate services including a venue for the wedding, she'd hadn't hesitated. Now she just wanted to make it as perfect as possible for them and everyone at Seabreeze Farm was pitching in. All she had to do was stop herself from crying, when Rose and Dave arrived to get ready for the wedding, and everything would be okay. She couldn't let the side down and get all emotional. Rose had strictly forbidden what she called 'unnecessary tears'.

'The cake's ready to go. Do you want me to take it over?'

Karen looked up from straightening the bride and groom on top of the cake as Ellie came into the kitchen.

'Aww, it looks great, Mum.'

Apparently Dave had bought Rose a bunch of yellow roses every Friday night since they'd got together, so the theme for the cake had been easy to come up with. It had three white cakes, with a layer of what Ellie would have sworn were real yellow roses between each one, if she hadn't seen her mother making them from sugar paste. Before they'd taken over the farm and transformed it into a wedding venue, Karen had run a small business from home making cakes, but now her skills were one of the farm's biggest draws and the cakes even had their own Instagram page with thousands of followers. Not that Karen got involved with that sort of thing if she could help it. She was far happier in the kitchen, which was just as well as that really wasn't Ellie's forte.

'Rose's daughter dropped the bridesmaids' dresses off last night and they're covered in yellow roses too. The barn is going to look amazing once we get the flowers in there.' Each of the tables would have a globe shaped glass vase filled with yellow roses as a centre piece and the theme was carried through to the bouquets and button holes. Rose had told them that each flower was like a ray of sunshine to her and she wanted the wedding to be bathed in sunshine, even if nothing could control the English weather, especially in early March.

'We just need to make sure that the gate to Gerald and Holly's field is double padlocked!' Karen grinned. Gerald was one of the donkeys who'd lived in the sanctuary long before they took over, and Holly was a sheep they'd rescued, who might only have three working legs but could still get herself into all sorts of trouble. They both had Houdini-like escapology skills and along with Dolly, the goat, they'd almost ruined the farm's very first wedding by eating all the flowers and the wedding cake on the morning of the ceremony.

'Ben's going around checking now and I'm not going to take the cake over until we're sure there's no chance of them or Dolly getting out.' Ellie could still feel her heart rate quicken when she thought about the panic that had set in on the day of the farm's first wedding, as she'd stood in the marquee surrounded by the wreckage that the escaped animals had left in their wake.

'Alan should be up here in a minute too. If he can tear himself away from Cliffview.' Karen laughed. 'He's obsessed with the place, although I suppose it could be worse, it could be another woman.'

Alan was Ellie's stepfather and he'd got together with her mother shortly after they took over the farm. Up until then he'd been a confirmed bachelor, who was proud of the fact that he hadn't bought any new clothes since 1992. He'd been frosty and unfriendly at first, but when they'd really got to know him, it had soon become obvious that he had a heart of gold. And Ellie couldn't imagine anyone less likely to have an affair.

While Alan's life – and wardrobe – had been transformed since he'd met Karen, he'd changed their lives too. After Ellie's father had let Karen down so badly, she'd deserved someone wonderful. Alan had more than lived up to the promises he'd made and he'd become the father that Ellie had never really had. So much so that she'd taken the decision to start calling him Dad and it had meant a lot to all of them. He'd also transformed Seabreeze Farm into the beautiful wedding venue it had become, all while running his own farm next door. He'd renovated some of the old farm buildings into holiday accommodation too, but his latest project was probably the most ambitious.

'When does he think it'll be ready?'

Cliffview was an old cabin that clung to the cliffs less than a hundred metres from the gates that led into Seabreeze Farm. When it had come up for sale by auction in January, Alan had been determined to buy it. No-one had been quite certain about the cabin's origins, but the best guess was that it had been a fisherman's hideaway, as it looked out over the Channel with uninterrupted views; except for the jungle of brambles that had almost obscured it completely by the time it came up for auction. It had been abandoned years before, and was only accessible by a narrow pathway littered with loose stones and the sort of potholes that a small dog could disappear into and never be seen again. The auctioneers had called it a 'project', but a condemned notice had seemed more realistic and Ellie hadn't been sure that even Alan could pull this particular trans-formation off.

'By Christmas he thinks, but he's determined to make it fully accessible, so he wants to offer it to one of the charities for a test run first. He'll probably speak to Steve from One Wish today, to see if anyone comes up on their list who might like to try it out in exchange for some feedback once it's ready. Hope-fully by the tail end of autumn.' Karen smiled again. 'Although he did say he was tempted to keep it as a play house for Mae, and Freya's children when they start to arrive.'

'He's already odds-on for granddad of the year award and I think the tree house he built for Mae's first birthday is more than enough, even if it will be a couple of years before we can let her go up there.' Alan had built a turret-shaped tree house for Ellie's daughter, with views every bit as amazing as the ones from Cliffview. Alan's daughter, Freya, would be getting married at the farm in December and she'd already told Ellie and Karen that she was planning on trying for a honeymoon baby. So Mae would have some company when she was finally big enough to make it into her tree house and there would be a whole new generation making the most of life at Seabreeze Farm. 'It's so lovely that he wants to make Cliffview accessible for everyone.'

'I think, since we've been helping out with One Wish, it's really opened his eyes to what some people have to go through. He keeps saying how lucky we are and I can't help agreeing, especially since Freya has come into our lives and we've had little Mae.' Karen slipped an arm around Ellie's waist, turning her towards the kitchen window. 'Just look at her, trotting up the path after her dad.'

'You're right, we're so lucky.' Ellie hugged her mother to her side, as she watched her fifteen-month-old daughter reach up to her daddy to be picked up. 'And I'm really glad One Wish have given us the chance to help out too.' Inheriting Seabreeze Farm had been life changing and so many wonderful things had happened since they'd taken over, it seemed only right to give something back.

'So am I. But if we're going to give Rose and Dave the best day possible, we'd better get going.'

'Yes boss.' Ellie smiled. She wanted to have a word with Steve from One Wish too, if she got the chance. This was their first wedding for the charity, but they'd already done some other things, including hosting a couple of animal keeper experience days. They'd had emails from the wish-fixers, thanking them for what they'd done for the charity so far, but the truth was that they got every bit as much out of it as the people whose wishes they'd granted, if not more. She wanted Steve to know that they'd be ready and willing to help out again whenever the opportunity arose, which turned out to be much sooner than anyone could have anticipated.

* * *

Georgia's heart felt as though it was racing, but for once she didn't have to worry whether it was a symptom of the looming heart failure that was threatening to creep into her life like the lengthening shadows as day turned into night. She knew exactly why. In five minutes, they'd be in one of her favourite places – Seabreeze Farm – and the harbour at Kelsea Bay was already visible from the winding coastal road that Gabe was currently navigating. Most people wouldn't get anywhere near this excited about a day out to somewhere they'd been so many times before, but with an illness that cut her off from so much, Georgia couldn't help it.

Her first visit to Seabreeze Farm had been back when she was four years old and her parents had taken her up to the donkey sanctuary, just before her father's accident. She'd had a thing about donkeys for as long as she could remember. It had all started with a book her father had read to her, that had belonged to him as a child, called *No-Good, the Dancing Donkey*. It was one of the only memories she had of her father and even that was vague, but her mother had continued to read the story to her long after her father's death. Ever since then, donkeys had been Georgia's favourite animals and their stubborn determination seemed to reflect the personality traits she'd had to develop over her lifetime, to get through the health issues she'd always refused to give in to.

Back then, Seabreeze Farm had been home to about twenty donkeys and it had been Georgia's idea of heaven. After that, whenever she'd had the chance – every birthday or special occasion when her mother suggested a treat – Georgia would ask if they could go to Seabreeze Farm. It was where her mother had taken her after she'd had to learn to inject herself with insulin, and where she'd gone after her first dialysis session. Just being there made everything better.

When it had been taken over and turned into a wedding and events venue, Georgia had been worried she might not get the chance to visit again. But a year or so ago, the owners had turned one of the converted outbuildings into a tearoom and it was even possible to visit the donkeys and other rescue animals in exchange for a donation to the RSPCA. Which meant, even though Georgia was on a horribly restricted diet as a result of the dialysis, she was back to taking every opportunity she could to visit Seabreeze Farm. So having the opportunity to accompany Gabe, to take photos at a One Wish wedding, was something she wouldn't miss for anything; even if it would probably leave her exhausted for the next couple of days.

'Are you okay?' Gabe turned to look at her as he stopped the car outside the main house at Seabreeze Farm. The courtyard had bunting in the shape of yellow roses hung between the farmhouse and the converted outbuilding that housed the tearoom on the opposite side. Just to the left of that was a pathway that led down to a converted stable block and the old barn, which was where the wedding was being held.

'I'm fine, just excited to be here again. Does that make me tragic?'

'No more than usual!' He laughed as she pulled a face of mock outrage.

'Well thanks very much, all your true feelings are coming out now!'

'There are a million things I could say about you, George, but tragic isn't one of them.' Gabe looked as if he was about to say something else, but then he shook it off. 'Are you ready?'

'Uh huh.' As Georgia got out of the car, she spotted yellow rose petals covering the pathway that led down to the barn, hiding the gravel beneath them. 'One Wish always do an incredible job, don't they?'

'They do, but Steve said a lot of the extras for this wedding are down to the owners of Seabreeze Farm. He said they've gone above and beyond with everything they've been involved in. I guess you've got to know them over so many years of coming here?'

'I knew Hilary, the aunt of the current owners, really well. Our shared obsession with donkeys bonded us despite there being a sixty-year age gap.' Georgia could still picture Hilary and the memory made her smile. She'd always found it easier to bond with older people. They were less likely to expect you to be able to hike Machu Picchu or party all night in Ibiza. Wandering around Seabreeze Farm, at her own pace, had always been Georgia's idea of the perfect getaway. 'Donkeys are a pretty niche fascination after all! I know Karen, Hilary's niece, who runs the tearoom, but I don't really know Karen's daughter, Ellie, although I've seen her around.'

'Ellie's lovely. She just seems to light up a room when she's in it.'

'It's a shame she's married to gorgeous super-vet Ben, then! He's Mum's hero for saving Barney's life when he had that obstruction.' She laughed. 'It's an age since you've had a girl-friend – I can't even remember the last time – and it's so like you to be attracted to someone who isn't available.' Georgia could never confess that she was secretly glad about that, at least while she was still around. But it worried her that it might never change and that Gabe would end up on his own forever. She just had to hope, that when she wasn't taking up so much of his time, he'd make it a priority to find someone who loved him as much as he deserved to be loved.

'I didn't mean it like that.' Gabe's tone had an edge to it, but he was probably just embarrassed at being caught out with a secret crush. 'I just meant she's got this amazing positive energy and she can't do enough for people, although Ben and the rest of the family are all the same.'

'Between them and One Wish they're going to give Rose and Dave an amazing day.' Picking up on Gabe's desire to change the subject, Georgia followed him down the path of yellow rose petals, both of them keeping to the edge to avoid disrupting the perfect scene.

Suddenly Gabe stopped and turned to look at her. 'Have you thought any more about the offer Steve made you?'

'There's nothing One Wish could do for me that I can't do for myself. I'd rather they spent their energies granting the wishes of those who really need them.' As much as Georgia admired the work the charity did, it wasn't for her. She didn't have any great dream to see the Northern Lights or ride the fastest rollercoaster in the world. And it was hard to plan a before-it-was-too-late wedding ceremony without anyone to marry.

'What about something from your not-a-bucket list?'

'The list is so small, it could probably fit into one of those tiny tin buckets they serve chips in at the Silver Seagull.'

'Are you sure they couldn't help you with anything? What's the one thing you want most?' Gabe tried to look nonchalant, but she was pretty sure he could have recited everything on the list word for word if he'd needed to, and in order of importance.

'Spending a summer living by the sea. I don't think even One Wish can make that happen without trawling through the Right Move rental alerts, the same way as I do every day. And I certainly don't want someone being guilt-tripped into renting me a house for a pittance. I'm not a charity case yet.'

'I know, I know!' Gabe held up his hands, as if he'd heard it all a hundred times before. And he probably had. There was nothing Georgia hated more than the suggestion that she couldn't do anything without someone else's help. It was bad enough that she was reliant on medication and machinery to keep her alive, she wasn't ready to accept that she couldn't make the most important of her dreams come true without help. She'd tick them off her not-a-bucket list, or she'd quite literally die trying.

'What about your other wish... for the puppy?'

'I just need to persuade Mum that a new puppy won't be too much for Barney. You're still okay to have the dog after I'm gone, aren't you?'

'I'm not going to need to do that.' Gabe looked at her again, reading the expression on her face. The last thing she wanted was for him to go into denial mode, like so many other people did when she tried to talk to them about the inevitable end that was on its way. It was happening, regardless of how much they tried to brush it off and pretend it wasn't.

'Gabe...'

'Okay, I promise, if it comes to that, I'll take the best care possible of your little dog. I'll be one of those people whose profile photos on Instagram are just of their dog and who call themselves its daddy.' Gabe grinned. 'Is that good enough for you?'

'Perfect.' Georgia reached up and planted a kiss on his cheek, leaning into him as he put an arm around her waist. She didn't want Gabe to forget about her, but she really wanted him to find happiness with someone else eventually. Having a dog was supposed to be a great way of meeting people and leaving that legacy meant she'd have a tiny part in his future, even after she was gone.

* * *

Rose and Dave were in the middle of the dancefloor surrounded by their family and friends. Rose might have needed a wheelchair for most of the day, and elbow crutches just to stand upright next to her new husband for their special song, but the smile on her face said it all. The wedding had been worth all the effort they'd put in, a hundred times over, and Ellie felt she'd finally earned a drink.

'Could you get me a glass of white wine when you get a minute please, Ross?' Ellie smiled at their regular Head Barman, who dipped his head to let her know he'd heard the request.

'Here you go, water in a wine glass with a twist of lemon.' Ross slid the drink across the bar to a woman about the same age as Ellie, if not a bit younger. Her skin was amazing, almost translucent, and she had incredible eyes that immediately made Ellie think of Audrey Hepburn.

'I know how to party, Ross, as you know only too well!' The woman grinned at him. 'But I'm going to have a big blow out one of these days, before it's too late.'

'Let me know when you do and I'll be there to serve whatever drinks you want, George.'

'I'll hold you to that. Give my love to your nan, won't you?' She reached out and touched his hand briefly as he nodded, and then turned and disappeared back into the crowd.

'Here you go, boss.' Seconds later, Ross handed Ellie the glass of wine she'd asked for.

'Thank you.' Trying and failing to keep her curiosity in check, Ellie leant across the bar. 'Who was that woman you just served? I've got a feeling I've seen her before, but I can't place her.'

'That's Georgia. Her family lived next door to my nan for years before she moved into sheltered accommodation. She comes up to the tearooms a lot, so you might know her from there.' Ross raised his eyebrows. 'Go on then, ask me what you want to ask.'

'What do you mean?' Ellie felt the heat rise up her neck. She was being nosy, but she couldn't help it, and Ross had caught her in the act.

'You want to know what's wrong with her, don't you? Why she said she'd have a blow out before it was too late?'

'I—' Ellie couldn't even deny it. There was no point; after two years of working together, Ross knew her too well for that.

'She's been diabetic since she was a kid, but over the years she's had a lot more complications than most people and the doctors struggled to get her blood sugar levels under control. Her kidneys got badly damaged and she ended up on dialysis, but even that wasn't straightforward and now they're telling her she's going into heart failure. Her mum told mine that they've only given her a year, unless she manages to get matched for a kidney and pancreas transplant. But she's got more complications than most people for getting a match and, with the limited time she's got before her heart can't handle a transplant, the odds are stacked against her.'

'Oh God, poor girl. How old is she?'

'Twenty-eight, but for heaven's sake don't have that sympathetic look on your face if you talk to her or she'll chuck her water over you.' Ross pulled a face. 'I told her once, when we were still at school, that I'd asked my teacher if we could do a sponsored walk to raise money for her treatment and she punched me on the arm!' Ross laughed at the memory.

'I take it she's not here to see what One Wish can do for her then?'

'Georgia would never accept that sort of help. She's here with Gabe, the photographer who covered the last One Wish animal keeper day. They're best mates from before we even met as kids. She's always loved Seabreeze Farm and she used to come up here to see the donkeys whenever she could, when it was still a sanctuary. She even dragged me along a couple of times when I was little, but it wasn't really my scene.'

'Oh okay.' Ellie's mind was already racing. Her heart went out to Georgia, but she could understand the reluctance of the other woman to be thought of as a victim. It wasn't the same thing, but she'd always hated anyone feeling sorry for her for having a father who couldn't be bothered to give her the time of day. She was still trying to think of something they could do for Georgia though, especially as she'd had a lifelong love affair with Seabreeze Farm. Even if she managed to think of something, they'd have to tread carefully based on what Ross had said. 'I'm glad Gabe's doing the photography again today. He's fabulous and it'll give Rose, Dave and their families some beautiful memories to look back on.'

'Talk of the devil, he's on the way over here.' Ross looked over her shoulder.

'What can we get you?' Ellie turned to Gabe and smiled. 'You've not stopped since you got here by the looks of things.'

'Just an orange juice, thanks, I need to keep my concentration levels up. I'm trying to capture every moment I can.' Gabe returned her smile. 'They're such a great family and there's so much laughter today, despite everything that's going on in the background. I really want the pictures to reflect that, so they can remember all of this when things aren't so great.'

'Ross said you've got an old friend helping you out?'

'He's probably also told you that Georgia and I have been joined at the hip for as long as he's known us? I can't really remember a time before her.' Gabe suddenly sounded wistful and Ellie didn't need to ask why.

'Ross mentioned that she's going through a tough time.' It was a massive understatement, but Ellie needed to gauge whether Gabe was as reluctant to talk about it as Georgia apparently was. 'He also said she loved Seabreeze Farm as a kid and I was wondering if there was anything we could do to... help out?'

'I'd love that, but George is a bit funny when it comes to gestures of any sort, let alone the grand variety, especially anything that might make someone feel sorry for her.' Gabe shrugged. 'But she still loves being up here and she comes up to your mum's tearoom whenever she can, so she can pop down and see Gerald and the others. She's got loads of photos with your aunt Hilary, I'm sure she'd love to show them to you.'

'That would be lovely. I know how she feels, too. Whenever I've got something on my mind and need to clear my head, I go down and spend some time with Gerald. He just has that sort of look on his face, as if he knows everything there is to know about the world, and somehow I always feel better after talking to him.'

'Even though he can't answer back?'

'Probably because of that!' Ellie laughed. 'Does Georgia live locally?'

'We both live in Chelford.' The town was about twenty minutes from Kelsea Bay. 'But we come here whenever we can and Ben is a bit of a legend to the whole family. His team was covering on call for one of the Chelford vets when Georgia's dog needed emergency surgery. Barney's like another child to Georgia's mum and she didn't stop talking about how brilliant Ben was for months. I think Caroline would have moved here just to be closer to Ben's surgery, but Georgia has always loved the place.'

'There is something special about being so close to the beach and, even though I wasn't born here, I can't imagine living anywhere else now. I love being able to see the sea every day.' It would have been easy for Ellie to take the life she had now for granted, but she never wanted that to happen.

'That's the one thing I wish Georgia would let me help her with. She really wants to spend the summer living somewhere with a view of the sea, but she can't afford the—'

'What about Kelsea Bay?' Ellie was already rushing ahead with the idea that had popped up out of nowhere and she cut in before Gabe had a chance to finish. She was sure Alan would go along with it, but there'd be a couple of huge hurdles to get out of the way first. Even if Georgia was prepared to agree to it.

'That would be perfect, but everything here is way out of her price range. Steve from One Wish has offered several times to rent somewhere for her for a month or so, but she doesn't do charity.'

'My stepdad, Alan, is renovating a house that's set right on the clifftop on the other side of the lane and he wants to make it fully accessible. The house looks straight out across the Channel to France.'

'She'd never be able to afford that.'

'What if she could have it for free?' Ellie put her hand up to stop Gabe, as he started to protest. 'The house will probably take Dad another nine months to renovate to a standard ready for rental, if he has to do it on his own alongside everything else. But if we could get One Wish to help get it ready in time for Georgia to stay there, it would be helping us as much as it helps her and he could start renting it out earlier. Maybe that way she'd see it differently?'

'Maybe.' Gabe screwed up his face. 'And I reckon Steve would be more than up for organising a sort of *DIY SOS* build if she agrees. But what about your stepdad?'

'Leave it with me.' Ellie was already moving away from the bar. Anything that provided a link back to her beloved aunt Hilary was amazing, and Ellie completely agreed with her mum about how lucky they were. Georgia had been dealt a much more difficult hand and if there was anything they could do to make that better, by drawing on Aunt Hilary's legacy, she wanted to do it. Convincing Alan would be the easy bit, but she had a feeling Gabe was going to have a much trickier task on his hands trying to persuade Georgia that this wasn't just another act of charity.

4

Georgia looked at the row of cakes displayed under spotless glass domes on the counter of Gerry's, the tearoom at Seabreeze Farm that was named after its most famous resident. They all looked gorgeous, but there were two that she would have loved to take a slice of, if it were possible. The first was described as Malteser cake. It had four layers of dark chocolate sponge, interspersed with butter cream the colour of light honeycomb, and on top there was a tightly packed layer of Maltesers nudging up against each other like commuters on the underground. Even without checking, Georgia knew it would be a definite no-no. The diet she'd had to follow since starting dialysis had made her diabetes diet seem like a walk in the park.

Next to the Malteser cake was a carrot cake and Georgia could smell the cinnamon and vanilla mingling in the air, making her mouth water. She wouldn't be able to have any of that either, but maybe she could persuade her mother to take a slice and she could enjoy the experience vicariously. Caroline was sticking pretty rigorously to her own diet, though, labouring under the futile hope of persuading the hospital team to allow her to donate a kidney, until a suitable pancreas could be found. Ethically it was something Georgia knew the hospital would never allow, but if it gave her mum something else to think about – other than the fact that the days were ticking past at a rate no-one could control – then it wasn't a bad thing. It would be good for Caroline's health, too. And more than anything, Georgia wanted her mother to find a way to be happy and healthy when this was all over.

Sometimes Georgia prayed for a donor. Not to God exactly, just anyone or anything that might be listening, but then she'd catch herself. To get the transplant she needed, someone else's life would have to end and the ripple effect of that would almost certainly devastate other lives. Except that wasn't the only reason she stopped herself from wishing for a donor; the truth was, she was terrified of having a transplant. While it could save her life, it was a huge operation and there was a big risk it might end things sooner than if they just let nature run its course. Despite all her attempts at stoicism, the thought of actually getting that call – saying what might be her final good-byes and being wheeled down to the operating theatre – scared the life out of her.

'Hello girls!' Karen greeted Georgia and Caroline like long lost friends, as she appeared from the back room behind the counter at Gerry's. 'What can I get you today?'

'Just a pot of tea.' Caroline sighed. 'I'm trying to stick to my diet and, of course, Georgia has to.'

'Mum!' Georgia gave her a gentle nudge with her elbow. She was never going to get the message that she didn't have to explain her daughter's back story to everyone she met. Not to mention that poor old Karen had heard it all several times before.

'Actually, the carrot cake is a recipe I found online and it's diabetes and kidney friendly.'

'You didn't need to do that.' Georgia smiled, but her face felt as if it was made of stone. She hated this; people feeling like they had to make special arrangements for her. Karen had probably had to slave over the cake for hours and it was bound to taste as though it had been made for someone on a restricted diet, so she'd probably have to chuck the rest in the bin when Georgia and Caroline left.

'I'm trying to extend my repertoire, with dairy free cakes for vegans and customers with allergies. I'm using some gluten-free recipes too, so this is just another string to my bow. Although I'm relying on some honest feedback, in case I need to go back to the drawing board.'

'I can't wait to try it, it looks fab!' Caroline reached out and squeezed Karen's hand. 'Thank you so much.'

'You're doing me a favour, honestly. More and more people are on sugar-free diets and I need to keep up to stay in business. I'll bring the tea and cake over to your usual table when it's ready. I reserved it when you said you'd be over today.'

Georgia let out a breath as she sat down at the table by the window, which was undoubtedly her favourite spot in Gerry's. You could see straight down to the field where the donkeys were currently grazing in the spring sunshine and, beyond that, there was a glimpse of the sea, which on a day like today looked almost as bright blue as the sky reflected in it. She was trying to hold her sense of irritation at bay, but it wasn't working. Seabreeze Farm was her happy place and just for one day she didn't want to be the girl with organ failure, whose clock was ticking down to zero right in front of her eyes.

'Did you call Karen to let her know we'd be coming in today?'

'No.' Caroline shook her head, emphasising her answer. 'I bumped into her at the farmer's market in Elverham on Friday and I told her we'd be in today, that's all. So you can stop bristling.'

'I'm not bristling.' Even as she said it, Georgia had to admit her mother was right. She'd felt the familiar tingling sensation at the roots of her hair when she'd thought her mother was turning her visit to Gerry's into some sort of special event, when all she craved was normality.

'Yes you are and you were doing it when Karen told you about the cake.' Caroline sighed. 'You do it every time Gabe tries to do something nice for you, too. You keep saying that you don't want everyone to treat you differently because you're ill, but the way you're acting, you're the one who's making this all about you.'

'What do you mean?' Georgia wanted to be indignant, but her mother never called her out like that unless she'd pushed it too far. Caroline was always on Georgia's side and, even before her mother answered, she knew she'd be right.

'You hate anyone helping you, or making special arrangements for you. Poor Steve from One Wish went away with a flea in his ear when he asked if there was anything the charity could do for you, and the look on your face when Karen mentioned the cake was frostier than any topping she could make.'

'I don't want people feeling sorry for me.' Georgia twisted the napkin into a knot.

'They just want to help! And doing something nice is as much about them as it is about you. People feel good when they can do something nice for you. It doesn't mean they think you're a charity case.' Caroline put a hand under her daughter's chin, forcing her to look up. 'You've got to let people in, otherwise we're all going to go mad watching you trying to battle this on your own.'

'I'm sorry.' Georgia let go of a long breath. 'It's just that after the blog started to take off, the comments that went with it were just so...' She couldn't finish the sentence in a way that made sense. Her mother was right, people meant well, but when you had so little time left to live, it was more important than ever that people let you experience *real* life, the way everyone else could. Not some sterilised, specially packaged version for the sick and dying. Sometimes that made Georgia prickly but she had to learn to rein it in. As much as it might feel like it, even the last year of her life wasn't just about her and she didn't want to make this even harder for the people who loved her than it already was.

'Here we go, girls, tea and carrot cake.' Karen set the tray down on the table and started to unload it.

'Have you got time to sit down with us?' Georgia smiled again and this time it didn't feeling like it was hurting her face. 'I mentioned to Ross, last time I saw him, that Mum and I had some photos from when I used to come up here as a child and your aunt Hilary is in lots of them. I thought you might like to see them?'

'I'd love that and it's quite quiet in here today, so Nicky can cover things unless a huge crowd suddenly arrives. I'll just go and grab another cup; we can't do this without tea!' Moments later, Karen was back at the table, taking a seat next to Caroline.

'This one was probably taken about twenty years ago.' Georgia slid a photograph across the table towards Karen. 'Your aunt was always so patient with me. She used to let me "help out", even though I was probably much more of a hindrance than a help! She also let me keep coming up for ages after she'd officially stopped running the place as a sanctuary. She was such a lovely lady.'

'She was.' Karen's face lit up as she looked down at the picture. 'She also knew how to recognise a kindred spirit and it's obvious she saw that in you. She could be quite a loner and often preferred the company of animals to people, but she definitely had a soft spot for you judging by these pictures.'

'When I first got diagnosed and I realised my life was always going to be different from other kids, coming up here was the only thing that made me feel better.' Georgia slid another photograph towards Karen. 'It was the same every time I got unwanted news from the doctors. Being up here, looking at the sea, always puts my problems into perspective and makes them seem so much smaller and less overwhelming. Listening to Gerald bray, in that wonderfully out of tune way only he can, and Jubilee calling back to answer him, never fails to make me laugh either. It's why I've always loved it so much.'

'Do you mind if I take a picture of some of the photos with my mobile? I'm sure Ellie would love to see them too.'

'There's no need. I had these copies made for you and there's a second set in here for Ellie.' Georgia handed over the wallet of photographs.

'Really? Oh my goodness, that's so kind of you.' Karen's smile was even broader now. 'These just mean so much. I haven't got nearly as many photos of Aunt Hilary as I'd like, and some of my happiest memories of growing up were spent on the farm. I know Ellie feels the same way.'

'It really is a wonderful place. Almost as good as this cake.' Caroline had already polished off the whole slice, in the time Karen and Georgia had been talking. 'I might need to stock pile it, so that I can have a treat when I need one. It will make sticking to my diet much easier. I'm determined that at my next check-up there'll be no sign of the diabetes and they'll change their minds about letting me donate a kidney to Georgia.'

'I don't want you to get fixated on that, Mum, because there's almost no chance they'll change their minds. Even if they do, it's not going to be enough. I'd rather you concentrated on finding someone who can make you smile again.' She must have said the same thing a hundred times already, but her mother didn't seem able to hear the words no matter how hard Georgia tried.

'It's got to be worth a shot.' Caroline turned towards Karen, ignoring Georgia. 'She needs a double transplant – a kidney and a pancreas – so that the diabetes doesn't destroy the new kidney too. The trouble is, there just aren't enough donors. The kidney bit is slightly easier, because they can use live donors. If they agree to me being one, it means she only has to be matched with a pancreas and at least it would buy her some time. Although it's a lot more difficult than I thought it would be.'

'Surely they'll let you if it's a match?' Karen furrowed her brow. 'Any mother would want to do the same for her child; I know I'd fight tooth and nail for the right to give Ellie my kidney if she needed one.'

'I make more antibodies than most people, which makes matching a donor harder. Even if they did let me use a live kidney donor, which they almost certainly won't, there's not much chance of getting a pancreas in time and I don't want to wish for that either. Not when it means someone else losing their life.' Georgia forced a shrug, uncomfortable about opening up to Karen this much. But her mother had got stuck into her favourite subject and the last thing she wanted was for Karen to encourage Caroline and inadvertently contribute to what was bound to be a bitter disappointment. 'I'd rather Mum helped me tick something else off my list and got married here at Seabreeze Farm, so that I can be a bridesmaid. I always pictured getting married here, if I ever met someone, even before you and Ellie turned it into a wedding venue. And Mum doing it would be the next best thing.'

'How's the dating going?' To her credit, Karen was clearly capable of realising that Georgia wanted to move the conversation on to something else and she didn't do what most people did and ask loads more questions about the transplant and the chances of it succeeding. It had been part of the reason why Georgia had started writing a blog in the first place, so she could direct people there for all the answers. She'd also wanted to connect with other people going through the same thing; they were the only people who really understood and who didn't immediately default to feeling sorry for her.

'I'm seeing someone who's really nice, but it's such early days and this one is putting a lot of pressure on me!' Caroline laughed, shaking off the talk of transplants and instantly looking ten years younger. 'I don't want to scare the poor guy off by telling him that my daughter's already booked in a wedding date for us here. Although I wouldn't put it past her.'

'I'll give you until the end of July to get your act together and book a date. After that I might have to take drastic action and speak to Ellie about making that booking!' Georgia was only half joking, but it wasn't about being part of a wedding at Seabreeze Farm. She just couldn't bear the thought of going and leaving her mum on her own; they'd been a team of two since she was four years old.

'We'll be here for you whenever you're ready.' Karen turned around as a large group of ramblers suddenly came through the door. 'I'd better get going before Nicky is rushed off her feet, but thanks so much again for the photos. And don't forget to let me know what you think of the cake, Georgia, when you get to try a piece.'

'I will and thank you for finding a recipe I could actually eat.'

'No problem at all.' As Karen disappeared back behind the counter, Georgia looked at her mother who was tapping the side of her nose.

'It felt good, didn't it?'

'What did?' Georgia furrowed her brow.

'Doing something nice for Karen and Ellie, by sorting out copies of the photos.'

'She did seem really pleased with them.'

'Uh huh and the nice feeling it gave you is exactly how other people feel when they do something for you. On the rare occasions that you let them.'

'Okay, okay, I get your point.' Georgia popped a piece of cake into her mouth and her taste buds immediately jumped into life. 'She's done a great job with this carrot cake too, so I can grudgingly admit that not every attempt to do things for me is a terrible idea. If Karen comes up with anything else, I promise to be a bit more grateful.'

'At least that's a start.' Caroline raised her eyebrows and Georgia glanced back over towards the counter, where Karen was talking to another customer. Whether the dating worked out for Caroline or not, one thing Georgia knew was that her mum could do with some good friends when she was gone. Having devoted so much of her life to looking after Georgia, Caroline didn't have as many of those as she should have done. It was time to add another goal to her not-a-bucket list and do everything she could to make sure Karen and her mum developed the sort of friendship that Georgia was sure they could. They had lots in common; both of them were loving and family orientated for a start. If the chance of them developing a friend-ship was reliant on spending even more time at Seabreeze Farm, that was just an added bonus.

* * *

Ellie kissed the top of Mae's head as she did up the straps in her high chair. The little girl was getting to the stage where she was determined to feed herself, even if that meant nothing within a ten-foot radius – including their little dog, Ginger – was safe from getting splattered with food. For the moment they should be okay, as Mae had a snack of rice crackers and strawberries, but it was amazing how difficult it could be to clear up half a punnet of strawberries that had been smooshed in between her daughter's chubby little fingers. She was a determined little girl, though, and once she made her mind up about something, there was no stopping her. A bit like her grandmother, who was currently wearing an expression of determination to rival anything Mae might adopt.

'What are you doing?' Ellie looked at her mother, who was sitting at the opposite end of the kitchen table from Mae. Karen used the kitchen at Seabreeze Farm for work, rather than the one in her farmhouse next door, as the oven was a lot bigger. When they'd first set up the wedding business, they'd put in an industrial sized oven and there were currently four cakes on the go, one for an upcoming wedding and the other three for Gerry's tearoom.

'I'm trying to work out how to post something on Insta-gram.' Karen let out a breath that made her fringe rise up. 'Why do these things have to be so complicated?'

'If you've got some cake pictures you want uploaded, I can

do it.' Ellie laughed. 'I thought we agreed it wasn't your area of expertise!'

'It's not, but there's something I want to do that isn't related to the business and I didn't want to have to ask you to add it to your to-do list, with all the events you've got coming up.' Her mum looked unusually serious.

'It's fine. I'm sure it'll only take a couple of minutes at most.' Ellie couldn't imagine why Karen would want to do anything on Instagram that wasn't related to the business. Her mother had mastered Facebook to a sufficient extent to keep in contact with distant relatives and had even re-established contact with friends she'd known from as far back as primary school. At almost thirty years younger, even Ellie wouldn't claim to be an expert on Instagram, or pretend to be that interested in it outside of a tool to advertise the business, come to that. So Karen's sudden determination to get to grips with it was baffling.

'It's not a one-off though. I want to start a campaign with one of those hashtag things. I think I've worked out how to do a campaign page on Facebook and I'm going to have a go at Twitter after I've worked out Instagram, but I'm not sure I'm doing it right.'

'What are you campaigning for?' If Ellie had been forced to guess, she'd have bet it would be something to do with bees. Both her mother and Alan were involved in a community project to encourage everyone with a garden space, even if it was a tiny window box, to plant seeds to grow wild flowers for the bees. They'd both donated substantial sums to the campaign organisers and her mother had even gone to a march dressed in a bumble bee costume. Alan had drawn the line at getting quite that involved, but it was undoubtedly a cause close to both of their hearts.

'Transplant awareness. I never realised until recently just how many people are waiting for a transplant and can't get one.' Karen looked up. 'I know the law is changing and people will soon be automatically considered as donors, but there's still a long way to go. If families are clear about their relatives' wishes, it makes the process a whole lot quicker and easier. Not to mention the fact that you can be a live kidney donor.'

'Is all of this for Georgia?' Ellie didn't need to wait for her mother's nod, it was obvious. Ellie had already put her own plan to help Georgia in motion and had arranged for Gabe to bring her up to Cliffview, to see if they could persuade her to stay there rent free for the summer. Steve from One Wish had agreed to call in help to get the necessary work done, if Georgia agreed. But from everything Gabe had said, that was a big if. When Karen had given Ellie the photographs of Aunt Hilary that Georgia had copied, it was obvious the young woman's story had touched Karen's heart too. Not to mention the empathy Karen felt for Georgia's mother, Caroline. Wanting to help was her default position, but that didn't mean Georgia would agree to be the focus of those efforts, no matter how good the intentions behind them were.

'I'm thinking of being tested myself, to see if my kidney is a match for anyone on the waiting list.'

'Have you spoken to Alan about this? It's not something to do on a whim, without thinking through the possible consequences. Especially given that the chances of that helping Georgia are incredibly low.' If it was selfish of Ellie to want to put a stop to her mother going down this road, then she couldn't help it. Glancing from Karen to Mae and back again, the feeling of being luckier than anyone deserved washed over her again. She wanted to hold on to it forever, which meant

Karen being around for as long as possible and Ellie would do whatever she could to make that happen.

'I know it won't help Georgia, but I can hardly front a campaign unless I put my money where my mouth is, can I? Either way, I'll certainly be putting my name on the register before it becomes mandatory.' Karen was wearing that look of determination again. 'It's all very well baking and decorating a cake in the shape of the transplant ribbon, but that's hardly likely to make big enough waves to find the donor Georgia needs.'

'Have you spoken to Georgia or Caroline about this? From what Ross and Gabe have told me, Georgia might not appreciate being the poster girl for a campaign. Even if it works.'

'I'm not naming Georgia in my campaign unless she gives permission, I'm just trying to raise the profile in the hope that someone will get added to the register who will be a match for her. Her consultant said the odds of finding a donor before her heart deteriorates too much, the way things stand, aren't much different to winning the lottery. Even if the campaign doesn't find a donor for Georgia, there must be thousands of other people in her position who the campaign might help.' Karen shook her head. 'I just keep looking at those pictures of Georgia with Aunt Hilary and I know she'd want us to try and do something. I can't keep counting my blessings but not helping someone who needs it.'

'You're always helping other people.' Ellie walked towards her mother, wrapping her arms around the older woman. 'And if I end up half the person you are, then I'll be happy.'

'You're much more than that already.' Karen leant her head against Ellie's. 'Alan's told me all about your plans for Cliffview.'

'I just hope we can persuade Georgia.' Ellie let go of her mother and picked up the mobile phone. 'In the meantime, let's get this Instagram page sorted and then I'll help you work out how to share the campaign on Twitter too.'

'I should have the transplant ribbon cake done by tonight. If I get some photos, that might be a good starting point.'

'Absolutely.' Ellie pushed down the worry that her mother might end up risking her own life to help a total stranger. It was the type of person Karen was, and she was never going to change. All Ellie could do was hope that the sacrifice Karen was prepared to make wouldn't be in vain, and suddenly persuading Georgia to stay at Cliffview for the rest of the summer seemed like the easy bit.

5

Georgia had guessed where they were going as soon as Gabe had taken the coastal road that led towards Kelsea Bay. Her mother was sitting in the back of the car and every time Georgia turned around to look at her, she was fiddling nervously with her seatbelt and biting her lip. Whatever was going on had set her mother on edge, and Gabe wasn't giving anything away.

'Surely you can tell me now where we're going?' Georgia had protested when he'd loaded the wheelchair into the back of the car. Despite the decorations they'd added in an attempt to personalise it, she still didn't want to take the wheelchair out unless she had to. She'd come to terms with how ill she was much more quickly than everyone around her, but that didn't mean she wanted to give in to the wheelchair when, for now, she was still able to walk short distances without it. She might as well have been wearing a giant label around her neck saying she was ill and it generated even more of the sympathetic looks she hated.

'Just be patient.' Gabe grinned and Georgia's stomach did

a little flip that had nothing to do with the twists and turns in the country roads. Sometimes, when you'd known someone for as long as Georgia had known Gabe, it was difficult to see how much they'd changed over the years. But just lately, Georgia had been noticing it more and more. If she'd met him now, she'd have been attracted to him straight away and it wouldn't have taken a slow burn of nearly two decades for her to eventually admit how she felt. For years she'd tried to convince herself that what she felt for him was the same deep, platonic love he'd always shown her, but her reaction the few times he'd had a girlfriend and it looked like it might be getting serious, told another story. Gabe had the most striking green eyes and a mouth that seemed to have a natural up-turn to it, which made it look like he was only ever a split second away from smiling. It was the opposite of a resting bitch face.

The first time she'd dreamed about kissing Gabe she'd been horrified and put it down to the craziness of the sub-conscious, something beyond control or explanation. Except recently she hadn't needed to even be asleep to think about Gabe in that way and she couldn't blame that on her sub-conscious. Now she was trying a different tack, blaming it on the fact that a life on dialysis meant she hadn't been on a date in forever. She'd have got her feelings for him out of her system a long time ago otherwise. But no-one wanted to date a girl who had to be hooked up to a machine every few days just to survive and who couldn't eat 90 per cent of the things on a restaurant menu, let alone head out for pre-dinner drinks. All of which meant that Gabe had become the unwitting object of her attraction.

'How long have you known me?' She kept her tone light, forcing herself to drag her eyes away from his face.

'Since we were a few weeks old. So, what's that, twenty-eight years?' Gabe lifted one hand off the steering wheel and ran it through his hair as she turned back to look at him.

'So that's basically forever, in terms of our lives, and you still don't know that patience isn't my strong point. I mean I can't even hang around and wait until I get to the top of the transplant list before I shuffle off.'

'I suppose that's the only reason you've stayed friends with me all this time, because it's not worth your while making new ones?' Gabe grinned. His ability to match her gallows' humour, joke for joke, was so unique, when everyone else seemed to tiptoe around the issue. Not that he couldn't be serious and support her when she needed it, or have moments when he seemed devastated by her prognosis, but that bit was easier. Finding someone to laugh at the absurdity of the whole situation was much more difficult and she never wanted to risk losing that.

'Georgia! Gabriel!' Caroline's tone was sharp and she gripped her daughter's shoulder. 'I know you think it's funny and it's your way of coping, but I really wish you wouldn't make jokes like that around me.'

'Sorry, Mum.' For a second she caught Gabe's eye and he grinned again. They'd been getting told off together for as long as either of them could remember and it was good to know that some things never changed.

'Just stop messing about and I'll tell you where we're headed. We're going to Seabreeze Farm.' Caroline blurted it out and Georgia could have sworn that Gabe's hands tightened on the steering wheel, making his knuckles go white.

'I'd kind of guessed we might be.' Georgia turned to look at her mother. 'But why all the secrecy? We've been going to Gerry's tearoom at least once a week since I had to give up work.'

'We're not going to the tearoom.' Caroline folded her arms across her chest, as if she'd already said more than she intended.

'Not another One Wish event, surely?' Georgia felt the roots of her hair start to prickle in that familiar way. If her mum and Gabe had set something up with the charity on her behalf, she wasn't going to be held responsible for her actions. She might struggle to catch her breath these days and be entirely reliant on dialysis to survive, but that didn't mean she wouldn't still resist every attempt to make her feel like a victim. Gabe and her mother knew that better than anyone.

'We're going to have a look at a house to see if you want to stay there for the summer.' There was a muscle twitching in Gabe's cheek, but Georgia would have known there was more to it even without the clue.

'There's no way I can afford to rent a holiday cottage at Seabreeze Farm. What's going on?'

'They're converting a cabin on the cliffs, on the opposite side of the lane from the farm.' Gabe's jawline was still tightly clenched, even as he spoke. 'They want to make this one fully accessible and put some reviews up online before they start to rent it out properly. They thought if you shared a review on your blog, it might help with advertising.'

'I find it very hard to believe that Seabreeze Farm would have any difficulty renting a new holiday let out. When I looked online there were pages of five-star reviews for The Old Stables and hardly any free weeks between now and this time next year.' Georgia wasn't a fool, there was definitely more to this than Gabe was letting on.

'Just talk to Alan and the others when we get there.' Gabe switched on the radio and turned his attention back to the road, making it very clear that the subject was closed.

It might be the end of the conversation for now, but if Gabe and her mother were up to something, Georgia was going to have plenty to say about it.

* * *

'Are you actually trying to kill me? Is that the plan? Bring me up to the clifftop, force me into the wheelchair and then tip me over the edge?' Georgia gripped the arm rests of the wheelchair, as Gabe continued to bump her down the rocky track that he'd promised led to Cliffview and not her untimely end.

'Sorry, but it's the only way to get down there at the moment and, until they sort it out, it's too steep for you to walk. Apparently the renovations are only part way through and sorting out the track is way down the list, but it would help if you'd wear your safety strap.'

'Yeah and it would help if I wore a crash helmet and knee pads, but I'm not doing that either.' Georgia would have folded her arms across her chest in a style her mother would have been proud of, if letting go of the arm rests had been an option. Caroline was up ahead of her, with Karen and Ellie, who had Mae, asleep, in a carrier on her back. None of this made sense. There was no way her mum would agree to her staying at Cliffview with access this poor and, as much as Georgia wanted to live in a house with a sea view, even for a couple of months, she didn't want it to be at the cost of all her independence. Just getting in and out for her dialysis treatment was going to be a nightmare if this was the only access to the cabin. It would be so hard to turn down the opportunity to stay here, though. Just looking out at the sea made Georgia feel free, even as she bumped along in her wheelchair with no control over its direction.

'Here we are. Excuse the mess.' Ellie waited for them at the bottom of a makeshift ramp, fashioned out of four lengths of scaffolding board, Mae still sleeping soundly in the carrier. 'Is this going to be okay for you to get the wheelchair up?'

'Thanks, but I can manage to walk from here.' Georgia was already pushing herself up from the chair, before anyone had the chance to protest. Thankfully her mother had already gone inside the cabin with Karen, and Gabe knew better than to argue with her.

'It's still a building site as you can see, but hopefully you can visualise how it will look when it's finished.' Ellie stepped back as Georgia got up from the chair. 'It's a big project, but you wouldn't believe what it looked like when Alan first took it on.'

'I'd camp in the middle of the rubble just for this view, if I could.' Georgia breathed in the sea air, tasting the salt on her lips. It really did feel as if just being here could cure everything and it was great that Ellie and her family were so determined to make it accessible. If they genuinely needed her help to make that happen, she'd do whatever it took, even if she wasn't around to see it come to fruition.

'Hopefully it won't come to you needing to camp.' Ellie turned towards the ramp. 'Shall we go inside, so you can meet my stepdad, Alan, and my husband, Ben? Then you can see where we're at with it.'

'Sounds good.' As Georgia took a step forward, Gabe reached out for her arm. He was long past asking if she needed his help, knowing her well enough to realise she'd more than likely bat him away, even if she did.

'Come on, George, you're keeping everyone waiting.' Gabe gave her a gentle nudge as he hooked his arm through hers and she saw Ellie's eyebrows shoot up in surprise, which made her laugh even more. Poor old Gabe was probably going to get a reputation for being really horrible, but she knew the truth and that was all that mattered.

'Wow, this is going to be fabulous.' Georgia caught her breath as they stepped on to the decked veranda outside the cabin. There was huge set of bi-fold doors on the front of the building, which were drawn back to expose the inside. It meant that there was an amazing view, whether you were in the open-plan living space, or out on the veranda. Georgia would have been happy to stay there forever, even though it was obvious that the inside was nowhere near ready.

'It's all down to my dad, Alan.' Ellie gestured towards the man kneeling on the floor, positioning a piece of the oak flooring into place. 'With help from Ben, of course. Ben, this is Georgia.'

'Pleased to meet you.' Ellie's husband had the same warmth in his smile as his wife and mother-in-law. They were such a lovely family and Georgia pushed down the twinge of envy that was rearing its ugly head. Ellie had it all. A lovely husband, a beautiful baby and a mother who was happily remarried to Alan, who sounded wonderful too. Two of those things definitely wouldn't happen for Georgia, but she hadn't given up on seeing her mum remarried to a good man yet. She'd fight for that one until the end if she had to.

'Great to meet you too, Ben. It looks like you've got your hands full with this project.'

'We're determined to get it right, but with just me and Alan working on it in our spare time, with help from Ellie and Karen when they can, it means progress is much slower than we'd like it to be.'

'I'd love to offer to help, but my DIY skills are more Homer Simpson than Bob the Builder.' Georgia turned towards Gabe. 'Although my friend here put together an

IKEA bookshelf all by himself and he only had to go to A&E once.'

'It wasn't A&E, it was the minor injuries unit.' Gabe laughed. If his pride was hurt by Georgia sharing an embarrassing story with Ben and Ellie, then he wasn't letting on. 'I lost one of the bags of screws, so I decided to try and staple gun the back panel on. Let's just say it didn't end well!'

'Sounds a bit like me when I first started out. I was more used to wielding a scalpel at the veterinary surgery when I first met Ellie, but Alan has taught me loads.' Ben glanced towards his father-in-law, who was getting to his feet.

Alan gave a small smile and held out his hand. 'Thanks for coming over, Georgia.'

'I didn't have a lot of choice. Mum and Gabe all but kidnapped me. Although I'm always happy to come up to Seabreeze Farm, but I've still got no idea what all of this is about.'

'Right.' Alan nodded, his face deadpan. He seemed like the sort of person who wouldn't beat around the bush and he didn't disappoint. 'We'd like you to stay here rent free for the summer, but your family don't think you'll agree to it.'

'They're right.' Georgia shook her head.

'But it wouldn't be charity.' Ellie's face was flushed. 'The thing is, it will take us months and months to finish this place on our own. But if you agree to stay here for the summer, then One Wish have said they'll help us finish the work. They'll bring a whole team in and have the work done within a fortnight and we'll be able to help so many more people, much more quickly than we could otherwise.'

'You're behind this, aren't you, Gabe? I've told you a hundred times that I don't need One Wish's help with anything. I'm not that desperate.' If Georgia had been able to storm off she would have done, but making it back to the veranda was about as far as her energy levels would take her. Turning on her heel, she walked slap bang into Steve from One Wish, who must have heard everything she'd said.

'Georgia, good to see you again.' Steve smiled. He had a hipster beard and a strange air of calm, which Georgia wouldn't have been surprised to hear came from meditating for three hours a day. Either way, his physical and spiritual presence had taken the wind out of her sails. 'Can you spare me a five-minute chat on the deck before you completely dismiss the idea of staying here for the summer?'

'I suppose.' Georgia knew she sounded like a petulant child, but it was too late to put an act on now.

'Come on then, let's talk.' Steve walked ahead of her and Georgia forced herself not to look back into the cabin when she reached his side. No doubt the others would all be whispering about her and making excuses for her rudeness, when there really weren't any acceptable reasons for it. Just because she was dying, it didn't give her the right to lash out at the people who were trying to help her. It annoyed the hell out of her that she hadn't found the balance yet between not playing the victim and pushing away the people she cared about the most. Maybe if Steve was as wise as he looked, he'd be able to help her find a way of finally doing that.

'I suppose you heard my outburst?'

'Uh huh.' Steve's tone was gentle. 'But it was nothing more than I expected, nothing more than any of us expected to be honest. The first time I met you and spoke about One Wish wanting to help you out with something, you almost tore my throat out. So I knew this wouldn't be a walk in the park.'

'I know I was rude, it's just that I have a hard time with people seeing me as poor little Georgia. *Oh look at her, bless her, dying so young. Let's do something for her.* Mum keeps telling me that people aren't just doing it because they feel sorry for me, they're doing it because it makes them feel good about themselves too. But it's not my job to make people feel good about themselves.'

'True.' Steve stroked his beard. 'But this project isn't about you. When the cabin is finished, with One Wish's help, Ellie and her family have agreed that the charity can use it for six weeks a year every year, providing we've got people who want to use it. The rest of the time it'll be available as a fully accessible cabin, to anyone who wants to book it, and there'll be substantial discounts for anyone who has a registered disability or ongoing illness. Don't you think everyone has the right to enjoy this sort of view?'

'Of course, but...'

'There are no buts. Just because you're ill, it doesn't mean you can't help other people, even after you're gone.' Steve shrugged. 'For One Wish to be able to step in and help out on this project, I've got to get it past the board of trustees. That means identifying someone who is eligible for one of our wishes, someone whose one wish is to spend the summer in a cabin overlooking the sea. It's not the kind of wish that has ever been sent to us before and, if you don't want it, Alan and Ben will have to finish the place on their own. That means spending more of their own money on getting it ready, money that could go to looking after the donkeys and other animals. It also means that One Wish won't be able to use it for six weeks every year from now on. Whether you agree to stay here or not, Ellie and her family won't make any money from the cabin until the autumn at the earliest, because it won't be ready without One Wish. You staying here and sharing the review on your blog is a winner for everyone, you've just got to swallow that famous pride of yours. If you can.'

'You'd already sold me on it when you said there'd be more money for the donkeys.' Georgia let go of a long breath, still not daring to turn around and look at the others, even though it felt as if there were several pairs of eyes boring into her back. Finishing Cliffview wasn't about her, it was about making this amazing place available to as many people who needed its beauty as possible, as quickly as they could. She just had to live with the fact that she'd be a One Wish recipient too, but she was doing it for Gerald and the other animals. As long as she could focus on making this about everyone but her, she might finally be able to swallow the pride that had been threatening to choke her – long before heart failure had its way.

6

Georgia closed her eyes and all she could hear was the sound of the waves crashing against the cliffs below as a brisk spring breeze made white horses dance on the surface of the water. She'd walked slowly down to Gerald's paddock at a pace that didn't leave her breathless, leaning on a gate post en route at least once to admire the view and catch her breath. Even taking things slowly had worn her out, so she'd been grateful to sit down on the picnic blanket she'd brought with her by the time she got there.

Despite the breeze, the April sun was warm on her face and she could quite easily have drifted off to sleep if Gerald hadn't suddenly started a cacophony of braying, louder than Georgia had ever heard before. It didn't seem possible that one small, elderly donkey could make quite that much noise. Georgia jolted at the suddenness of the sound, her sketch pad sliding off her lap. When she looked up, the cause of Gerald's outburst was obvious; Ellie was walking across the field towards them carrying what Georgia could only guess was a bucket of feed. The old donkey seemed certain it was and he had a turn of speed that was even more surprising than the volume he was capable of achieving, when he put his mind to it.

'God, sorry, I didn't realise you were down here. I've got to stop carrying the donkeys' hard feed in a bucket, so Gerald can't hear me coming before he even catches sight of me.'

'Does he always make that much noise?' Georgia laughed as Gerald flattened down his ears and launched into another ear-splitting bray, bearing his big yellow teeth at the other donkeys so they knew exactly who was first in the dinner queue.

'Pretty much, but at least he finally seems to have stopped breaking out of the paddock in search of food. He's a pain in the you-know-what, but luckily it's impossible not to love him anyway.' Ellie rolled her eyes. 'Did you manage to get any sketching done?'

'Gerald was proving to be the perfect muse. It's been so lovely spending the afternoon out here, I can't thank you enough for letting me come over. I already feel like I owe you a mountain of gratitude for the Cliffview project, let alone this on top of everything else.'

'You don't owe me anything.' Ellie tipped the bucket of feed in a line along the inside of the paddock fence, which meant, despite his best efforts, Gerald couldn't hog it all to himself. 'You're the one doing us a favour by using your wish to get the project finished. I popped down there earlier and it's like a scene from *DIY SOS*. Although I think Alan is glad Nick Knowles isn't involved; he's been Mum's pin up for years. She even loves his music. I suppose someone has to!'

'Surely not even Nick Knowles could turn her head when she's got Alan? He's such a great guy. When I apologised for reacting the way I did about staying at Cliffview for the summer, he was so understanding.' Georgia still felt herself go hot at the memory. She was mortified that her fight to stay independent for as long as possible might have made truly good people feel bad. Not to mention the fact that it would have meant missing out on the chance to fulfil one of her dreams. The moment she'd stood on the veranda at Cliffview, she'd fallen in love. And if there really was such a thing as heaven, Georgia wanted it to be exactly like that. Either way, she'd be getting her own slice of heaven and it was down to people who were putting a complete stranger like her before themselves.

'I don't think she'd look twice at anyone else, even Nick Knowles. She'd have me to answer to if she did. Alan's been the most amazing stepdad and no-one dotes on Mae more than him. He's a bit of a hero as far as I'm concerned and I'm proud to be able to call him my dad.' Ellie raked a hand through her hair. 'Although, talking of heroes, when I was over at the cabin earlier, Gabe was really getting stuck in with helping out. Steve from One Wish told me that he's been doing family portrait photo sessions in exchange for donations to the charity, as well. He's been booked back to back apparently.'

'And there was me thinking he was just making excuses not to see me.' Georgia felt the tension, which she hadn't even realised she'd been holding in her shoulders, drain away. Gabe had definitely been a lot quieter and a lot less available in the week since he'd first taken her to look at Cliffview. She'd put it down to him being annoyed at how she'd acted, when he'd worked so hard to make it happen, but it seemed she'd been wrong about that too.

'Gabe's lovely. He's going to make some girl really lucky one of these days.' Georgia swallowed the lump that had suddenly formed in her throat. Since Steve had talked some sense into her at Cliffview, she couldn't help feeling more selfish than ever for wanting Gabe to wait until she was out of the picture before starting a relationship with anyone; when there'd be no risk that seeing him with someone else would make it feel like she had a knife in her heart. The fact that he'd only ever seen them as friends was painful enough, without having to watch him fall in love with someone else.

'He told me how lovely you were too. Sounds like you could be made for each other.' Ellie's eyes met hers for a moment and Georgia shook her head. If Ellie had misread the depth of their friendship for something else, then she wouldn't be the first. But it was up to Georgia to squash that idea before there was even the tiniest risk of her starting to believe it might be true.

'We're just the oldest of old friends, that's all, and we know each other inside out. I guess that's a version of soulmates, though, isn't it? Even if there's absolutely no hint of romance.'

'Soulmates come in all sorts of forms.' Ellie rubbed Gerald's head as he nudged into her side, rooting around for the possibility of an extra hidden supply of donkey feed. 'Gerald here was my aunt Hilary's soulmate, at least for the last part of her life, and he made her so happy. I don't think it matters who we love as long as it adds something to our lives. Even Mum's crush on Nick Knowles has a purpose, because she says she always feels better after having a good cry at an episode of *DIY SOS* and it makes her realise just how lucky she is all over again. It's why she always wants to help One Wish – why we all do.'

'I'm amazed so many people have been willing to get involved in the Cliffview project so quickly. I never dreamt they'd get such an amazing response. I just wish I could do something to help, but even standing outside a shop shaking a collection tin all day would probably have me flat on my back. All I'm good for is sitting here and sketching.' Georgia flipped open her sketch pad and Ellie gave an audible intake of breath.

'Oh wow, that's amazing, you've captured Gerald's character perfectly! Are there any others? Can I have a look?'

'Help yourself.' Georgia handed her the sketch pad. Since Ellie and her family had given her free run of the farm, she'd felt more inspired to draw and paint than she had in years. The thought of being able to sit on the deck outside Cliffview and paint, looking at the amazing view it offered, gave her a warm feeling in the pit of her stomach. In her fantasy, Georgia imagined Gabe being there too, taking amazing photos, as the sun set and rose over the Channel below them. He hadn't mentioned staying with her and, even if he did, he wouldn't be with her in the way Ellie might have imagined. There was too much at stake to risk that.

In the unlikely event that Gabe had somehow been suppressing his feelings for her for years, then giving in to them would only hurt him more when she died. And if he didn't feel the same as Georgia, telling him she loved him would be awkward for them both and pile on the sense of loss she already felt about having to say goodbye. She'd coped with each diagnosis over the years by learning to live in the moment and trying not to grieve for the things she couldn't do, or couldn't have, by fighting to retain control of the things she could. That meant she could carry on being Gabe's best friend, just as she had for nearly thirty years, and celebrate having whatever time they had left together. Ellie was right, soulmates came in all forms and she'd been lucky to have had so many years with Gabe.

'These pictures are amazing. The one of Dolly looks like she's about to start talking at any minute and telling the story of her latest escapade.' Ellie smiled as she looked down at the sketch of the farm's resident goat, whose latest escape had apparently involved eating the Britain in Bloom display at the entrance to the harbour. Ellie and Ben had tried everything to keep her contained but, unlike Gerald, she was still working hard to be the world escapology champion.

Ellie had already told Georgia that the only way to guarantee Dolly wouldn't escape, was to put her in the stable and bolt the top door, as well as the bottom, which seemed far too cruel as a permanent solution. Chaining her up in the field wasn't an option Ellie and Ben wanted to consider either, but luckily the residents of Kelsea Bay had grown pretty relaxed about Dolly's adventures over the years and she'd become the unofficial mascot of the town, with a reputation that had spread on the internet. Whitstable might have been the number one seaside town on the Kent coast for attracting famous second home owners, but Kelsea Bay had its own celebrity in Dolly.

'All the animals have so much character, but especially Dolly, Gerald and Holly, and the stories you and your mum have told me about them make me smile whenever I think of them.'

'They're so naughty, but somehow it just makes me love them all the more.' Ellie flicked over another page in the notepad. 'People are always asking about the three of them and they must be the most photographed farm animals in the country. I think if we had some sort of merchandise with their images on, it would sell really well. But organising it has never made it to the top of my to-do list.'

'Would you do it to raise money for the farm?'

'No, we're doing fine now thankfully. When we first started, things were tight and if we hadn't had Ben's salary as a vet, plus the income from Alan's arable farming, I think we'd have gone under before the business had the chance to take off. But since then the wedding and events bookings have started to come in thick and fast, and both the tearoom and holiday lets have been incredibly busy too. We've been so lucky.'

'I've got a feeling it has more to do with hard work than luck.'

'Maybe, but we've loved every minute of it. When I think back to commuting up and down to London and working in a soulless job at a bank, I still have to pinch myself that I'm here every day and this is my office. If we could get some merchandise with the animals on, I'd love to raise money for One Wish.'

'Me too.' Georgia didn't miss the look of surprise that crossed Ellie's face. 'I know I've been a bit resistant to their help, to put it mildly. But that doesn't mean I don't realise what an amazing job they do. When I was at Dave and Rose's wedding with Gabe, I could see how much the day meant to them and their families, and I've watched the videos online of them sending children to Disney to make memories they wouldn't have had the chance to make otherwise. Do you think if I finished the pictures of Gerald and the others, and added some colour, they might work as postcards or something to sell in Gerry's tearooms? I know it won't raise a fortune, or change the world, but at least it'll feel like I'm doing something to contribute.'

'That's a great idea!' Georgia could almost see the cogs in Ellie's mind turning over. 'I think printing them on T-shirts, mugs and tea towels would be winner too. Dolly's got her own Facebook and Instagram page that Ben set up to document her antics and raise the profile of the farm, so we could probably sell some stuff online.'

'Do you really think there'd be a demand for them?' Georgia felt a frisson of excitement at the prospect of doing something to help, by sharing something she loved. It would also tick off the second big goal on her not-a-bucket list and raise some money for charity. Being at Seabreeze Farm was starting to make the impossible feel possible again.

* * *

Caroline grasped Richard's hand as they followed Georgia and Gabe down the path towards Cliffview. This was their fifth date and holding hands already felt completely natural, so it wasn't the reason she was shaking. That was down to the anticipation of how Georgia might react when she saw the finished version of Cliffview. Everyone had worked so hard to get the project finished and when Richard had given up his weekend to pitch in too, Caroline had finally begun to let herself imagine that things might go beyond a few dates, which she'd only agreed to in the first place to keep Georgia quiet. It was difficult to think too far into the future, when there was a good chance that any future beyond this year might not contain her beloved daughter. But she was trying to take a leaf out of Georgia's book and live in the now.

Ellie, Karen and the rest of their family had been even more amazing than Steve and the team at One Wish. Karen had worked hard to master the social media accounts that she'd apparently had almost no interest in, before trying to raise the profile of the transplant waiting list. She'd signed up for testing as a live kidney donor, as had Alan and Ben. Ellie would probably have done it too, if she hadn't had an announcement of her own that she was waiting until after the big unveil at Cliffview to reveal. Karen had shared the news of Ellie's pregnancy with Caroline, though, and in a very short time the two women had become incredibly close. Karen instinctively understood how Caroline felt about Georgia, having raised Ellie for years on her own too. They'd both been in a team of two, mothers and daughters against the world, and Karen already felt like a friend for life.

'If the work they've done to sort out the path is anything to go by, then the cabin's going to be amazing.' Georgia's voice carried in the night air and Caroline could hear her daughter's excitement. Ever since she'd agreed to spend the summer living at Cliffview and had started coming up to Seabreeze Farm on an almost daily basis, it was like a light had been switched on inside her again.

'It's definitely easier to get down the pathway now it's not just loose rocks and shingle. Saves me having to work out to try and get big enough muscles to push you up and down to the cabin several times a day. I'd have been like The Rock by the end of the summer.' Gabe laughed as Georgia reached out and grabbed his wrist.

'Are you calling me fat?'

Given that a strong gust of wind could probably have blown Georgia off her feet, it was obvious that Gabe was joking. He and Georgia were just doing what they always did. He'd perfected the art of making Georgia smile when no-one else could, as easily as he'd taken to being able to inject Georgia with insulin if he'd needed to, after she'd had a hypo, and stepping in to drive her to and from the hospital for dialysis if Caroline couldn't do it. The only time Caroline couldn't deal with the joking was when it was about Georgia dying. Some things just couldn't be laughed at, even if Georgia claimed it made it easier to accept. That was probably where they differed the most. Caroline would *never* learn to accept that Georgia was dying. You weren't supposed to bury your child and she'd fight with everything she had to make sure it didn't happen, even if she had to hide half her efforts from Georgia.

'I wouldn't dare call you fat. Like your mum, I know better than to get on the wrong side of you.' Gabe turned and smiled at Caroline, and she couldn't stop the thought that suddenly popped into her head as she looked at the man who'd become like a son to her over the years: would she lose him too when Georgia was gone?

'Too right, just keep remembering your place.' It was Georgia's turn to laugh. 'Anyway, you won't be around to push me up and down the path all day long, even if I needed you to. I can hardly expect you to jump into your car and drive down to Kelsea Bay every time I want to leave the cabin, can I?'

'I was going to ask you later, but I was thinking I might stay with you at the cabin, if you don't mind?' Gabe kept his tone light and Caroline felt as if a weight had been lifted from her shoulders. The prospect of Georgia being alone here every night had made her feel like hyperventilating, but her daughter would never have agreed to Caroline staying with her. This was her chance to be like every other twenty-eight-year-old woman and live an independent life. Caroline had been planning on trying to persuade Georgia to take Barney to the cabin for company, but Gabe was a far better solution than the dog. She just had to hope Georgia would agree.

'That's fine, if it doesn't interfere with work?' Georgia was keeping her tone equally light, but Caroline had seen the way she looked at Gabe when she didn't realise anyone was watching. She might protest that they were just friends until the last, but Caroline was sure her feelings went beyond that. It was something else she didn't want to spend too much time dwelling on. Falling in love and getting married was just one more thing Georgia wouldn't get the chance to experience if they didn't find a donor, it was why she was so keen to live the experience vicariously through Caroline. That put pressure on a relationship, even one that felt as promising as the relationship she was developing with Richard. He'd probably collapse in a heap if she told him that Georgia was determined to see them married off by the autumn.

'Most of my upcoming assignments are local to Kelsea Bay. I've got three weddings at Seabreeze Farm alone over the next month.'

'So that's why you want to live with me, is it? Just free bed and board?'

'I thought I could do some cooking for you?'

'I'm not eating anything you cook! The last time you made me dinner, we had to smash the smoke detector off the ceiling just to get it to stop.'

'Okay, maybe I won't cook then, but I'm much better at keeping the place tidy than you. Remember when the caretaker in our halls refused to go into your room, because of the state it was in?'

'I've got a bit more domesticated since then!'

'Luckily I'm not after you for your cleaning skills. You've got other qualities. For a start, you've got a great eye for helping me pick out my best shots, so I suppose I can put up with the rest.' Gabe dropped a kiss on the top of Georgia's head as they finally reached the bottom of the wooden ramp that led up to the cabin. 'Right, we're here. Are you ready?'

'They're not going to make too big a thing of this, are they?' Georgia turned to look at Caroline, as she and Richard drew level with the bottom of the ramp.

'They want to get a bit of advertising for One Wish and the farm, so I think there's going to be a speech and Gabe's going to take some photos, aren't you?' Caroline needed Gabe's back up on this. Any fuss was too much fuss for Georgia, but it was the least they could do to say thank you.

'Yes, they want some pictures for both social media accounts and you can always use them on your blog, when you post your review at the end of the summer.'

'Maybe I should have brought the wheelchair and stayed in

it all night then, giving everyone the sort of Tiny Tim look that would illicit a few more donations.' Georgia sucked in her cheeks and did her best to look as pathetic as possible, but it just ended up causing a coughing fit.

'Maybe not.' Gabe linked his arm through hers again, starting up the ramp. 'Because you're much more like another sort of Dickens' character.'

'Oliver Twist?' Georgia said, as they reached the top of the ramp.

'I was thinking more of a bit part, you know... Victorian prostitute with emphysema? That sort of thing!'

'You know exactly how to make a girl feel good on a special occasion.' Georgia laughed again and Richard raised his eyebrows.

'Sorry, they're like this all the time, but deep down they love each other really.' Caroline smiled at Richard as the bi-fold doors to the cabin were drawn back and the small crowd inside started to cheer.

'They're great and so are you.' Richard took hold of her hand again and she was doubly glad she'd asked him to come along. She had to be careful, though. She hadn't let herself rely on anyone since Georgia's father had died and she couldn't risk letting herself get too close, not when she was already being forced to contemplate losing the most important thing in her life.

* * *

Ellie wanted to make sure everyone had a glass of something to toast the team who'd helped complete the project, before she made the speech to thank them all.

'Can I get you a top up, Caroline?' She filled the older woman's glass, as Caroline nodded.

'Thank you and thank you so much for everything, the place looks amazing. I was just telling your mum and Alan that it's like a dream come true for Georgia, even if she might not show it.'

'She hasn't stopped smiling all night and that's more than enough for me and Karen.' Ellie's stepfather put an arm around his wife as he spoke. 'Not to mention the fact that Georgia has also thanked us at least ten times, but the look on her face says more than words ever could.'

'She's always wanted to live in a house where she could look out of the window and see the sea. It was one of the things she was determined to achieve when the consultant told her to do the things she wants to do while she can.' Caroline's voice caught on the final part of the sentence. 'I'd applied for a loan to cover the cost of renting somewhere and I was trying to work out how to get Georgia to agree to something like that, when you and One Wish stepped in. Even if I had managed to persuade her, I don't think we'd have ever found somewhere as lovely as this.'

'And we wouldn't have got it finished for ages, or to this standard of accessibility, if Georgia hadn't used her One Wish offer on it. So that makes us even.' Karen clinked her glass against Caroline's. 'And that was before she did such amazing pictures of Holly, Gerald and Dolly.'

'She hasn't let me see them yet!' Caroline shook her head. 'But she started drawing as soon as she could pick up a pencil and I think it's what's kept her sane through all the hospital stays over the years. I can't wait to see the pictures of Gerald; I swear to God he actually tries to talk to me when I go down to his paddock.'

'Knowing Gerald, he's probably asking if you've got any treats in your pocket!' Ellie grinned. 'Right, if everyone's got a drink, I'll just finish doing the rounds before I make the speech. Unless you've changed your mind and want to do it, Dad?'

'I'd rather break my thumb with a hammer all over again.' Alan lifted up his bandaged hand, which was covering the injury he'd sustained on the second to last day of the project. He might look like he was joking, but Ellie knew him well enough to believe it was true; Alan would take physical pain over the embarrassment of having to make a speech any day.

'Okay, I'll take it on the chin then.' Picking up another bottle of champagne from the kitchen island, Ellie headed back into the crowd to top up the last few empty glasses.

'Are you ready?' Ben walked towards her and she nodded. There were dark shadows under his eyes from working long hours at the surgery, as well as helping out on the project whenever he could. Ellie would have liked to do more of the physical work herself, but discovering she was pregnant again meant she couldn't push herself too hard. It had been tiring enough keeping everything running at the farm with the chronic indigestion that seemed to have arrived the moment the pregnancy had been confirmed. It would all be worth it in the end, but there was far too much going on to give in to tiredness. By June she'd be in the second trimester and she'd felt so much better at that stage with Mae. She'd also feel more comfortable about spreading the news more widely when she'd passed the so-called danger zone. She just hoped no-one thought she was being lazy in the meantime by not helping out much.

'Luckily I don't think anyone will be desperate for me to make a lengthy speech and, as long as I get the chance to thank everyone and advertise the fundraising efforts for One Wish,

I'll be happy.'

'Excuse me, can I just say something?' Georgia had taken the words right out of Ellie's mouth and Gabe was knocking heavily against the top of the kitchen island to get everyone's attention. A few seconds later every pair of eyes in the room were focused on Georgia. 'I just wanted to take the opportunity to thank everyone who has made this happen and given me the opportunity to fulfil the dream of living in a house that over-looks the sea. I probably won't be able to name everyone, but I'd like to highlight some really special people including Steve and his team of volunteers from One Wish, Alan, Karen, Ellie and Ben from Seabreeze Farm, and their other friends and family, including Liv and Seth, and Freya and Ollie who I'm told have taken a week of annual leave just to help out. Amazing! I'd also like to thank my mum, Caroline, and her partner, Richard, for getting stuck in, as well as my best friend, Gabe, for his work on the project, his fundraising efforts and most of all for persuading me to swallow my pride and take up this wonderful opportunity. You're all truly incredible people and I could never thank you enough, so instead I'm just going to say cheers.' Georgia raised her glass, which Ellie had topped up with fizzy water in lieu of champagne, as everyone joined in the toast.

'Thank you, Georgia, that was perfect and it saved me my least favourite job of public speaking!' Ellie stepped forward whilst they still had everyone's attention. 'There's just one more thing I wanted to add and that's to thank you, Georgia, for sharing some of your incredible art work with us and allowing us to use it to raise some funds for One Wish.'

'Ta da!' Just as rehearsed, all of the crew who'd worked on the project at Cliffview opened the jackets they'd been wearing to reveal T-shirts with a reproduction of the picture Georgia had drawn of Gerald on the front. Ellie had got thirty T-shirts made in a print shop in Elverham, but there was a much bigger order in for a series of different designs on not only T-shirts, but sweatshirts, mugs, coasters and tea towels. Ellie was covering the cost of the initial order, so everything they made would be pure profit for One Wish.

'They look great!' Georgia stepped back to look at the shirt Gabe was wearing. 'I'm just so glad I can do something to pay back the huge debt I owe you all.'

'To One Wish and Seabreeze Farm!' Gabe held up his glass and everyone joined in the toast all over again.

Ellie took a sip of her own fizzy water and, as she put down her glass, she caught Karen's eye. It had been a great evening, but her mother was clearly struggling not to cry and Ellie didn't need to ask why. When the summer came to an end, things would go back to normal for them and Cliffview would be empty and ready to rent out. But Georgia would be gone, possibly forever. If all the fundraising and campaigning for organ donation didn't do the trick, then it wouldn't be for want of them trying. They had to give it all they'd got, because it was the only chance Georgia had.

7

Georgia watched the sail boat gliding across the water that stretched below the veranda of Cliffview as it headed towards the French coast.

Before her diabetes had affected her kidneys so badly that she'd reached end-stage kidney disease, which necessitated visits to the hospital every few days, Georgia and Gabe had often taken the chance to hop across the Channel for a day out in France or Belgium.

The last time they'd gone, they'd spent the day in Bruges, walking around and marvelling at the beautiful architecture, with houses that looked as though they could have been carved from ginger bread. After an hour or so, they'd stopped outside a coffee shop to indulge in handmade chocolates with their coffee, before drifting down the canals on a tourist boat and having lunch in the beautiful main square. If she really thought about it, she could still taste the Dame Blanche, a dessert made from delicious vanilla ice cream, whipped cream, and warm molten chocolate. That sort of thing was off the menu on her dialysis diet, but maybe next time she ventured down to the harbour with Gabe, they could pick up some mussels to recreate the main course and pretend that the veranda at the cabin was that restaurant in the main square in Bruges.

Something about being at Cliffview made it feel like the world had opened up to Georgia again, even if she had to stay within half an hour of the hospital. Putting her stubbornness to one side, and letting One Wish and Seabreeze Farm fulfil her dream of spending her last summer by the sea, was one of the best decisions she'd ever made.

'I'm not interrupting anything am I?' Ellie called out from the bottom of the slope that led up to the veranda. 'Sorry, I didn't want to make you jump by just coming straight up.'

'Come up. You're not interrupting at all and it's just as well you turned up, otherwise I might have dropped off again. I'm supposed to be finishing a couple more paintings while Gabe is out working, but this view is hard to drag my eyes away from. I feel like one of those people who's supposed to be working from home, who gets endlessly distracted by day-time TV. Although this is a much better way to waste my time.'

'I read something the other day about day dreaming being really important.' Ellie stepped onto the veranda. 'Apparently it's the first stage of making your dreams come true and women don't do nearly enough of it compared to men. So I'd suggest staring at the view for a good couple of hours every day, at least, and calling it part of the *creative process*. I used to wander down to the fields and talk to Gerald and the others about the plans I had to turn the farm into a wedding venue when we first moved in. Some people would have called that time wasting, but it was what got me through the really stressful times when we weren't sure if we'd end up losing the farm.'

'I'd talk to the animals all the time if I lived at the farm. I talk to Mum's dog, Barney, too, and it always helps me to think things through.' Georgia smiled and indicated for Ellie to join her at the table on the veranda, where she sat whenever it was warm enough. 'I absolutely love it here, but I do miss Mum and Barney.'

'I know it's not the same, but I can always lend you my dog, Ginger, if you'd like some canine company? Although she's a well-known cake thief, so you'll just have to keep her away from this.' Ellie lifted the lid off the cake tin she'd set down on the table in front of her. 'Mum got the recipe from a kidney care website in the US. They're molten mint chocolate brownies apparently and she's taped the recipe to the bottom of the tin, so you can double check the ingredients if you're worried about anything.'

'That's amazing! If I didn't know better, I'd say your mum had mystical powers. I was just thinking about a dessert Gabe and I had in Bruges, last time we were able to get over there, which had molten chocolate poured all over the top. I had no idea I could have anything even close to that on my dialysis diet, so I love your mum more than ever, if that's even possible.'

'She's great, but then so is your mum. How are things going between her and Richard?'

'Pretty good, but she spends so much of her time focusing on me that I worry she won't put enough into her relationship with Richard to make it last.' It would be a huge relief knowing her mother had someone who made her their absolute priority and who would be there to support her once Georgia was gone. Leaving her mother might even be a tiny bit easier, because right now she couldn't bear the thought.

'Are you really hoping that they'll get married by the end of the summer?' Ellie kept her tone even, but Georgia didn't miss the furrowing of her new friend's brow.

'No, not really.' She grinned, picturing the look of horror on her mum's face every time she mentioned it. 'I wouldn't want to put that much pressure on her, even if I would like the chance to be a bridesmaid at Seabreeze Farm, seeing as I'll never get to have a wedding here myself. All I really want is to be able to go believing she's found someone she could make a life with, someone she can lean on when things get tough.'

'Richard certainly seems like a good guy and he didn't even have to be asked before he volunteered to help finish the cabin. Although I'm sure there are brides we've got booked in who'd be more than happy to have an extra bridesmaid, if we explained.'

'Oh God, no! I'd hate to gate crash someone else's wedding like that.' Georgia shook her head. 'I said it more as a joke at first, to guilt trip Mum into signing up to the dating app and force her into taking the first step to moving on. Now that I'm staying here until September, she's got some breathing space to spend time with Richard. I'm getting to spy on lots of Seabreeze Farm weddings too, just by being up here for the summer, so that's more than enough for me. Shall we try one of these brownies with a cup of tea, if you've got time?'

'I've always got time for tea and cake, although that's not the only reason for my rapidly expanding waistline.' Ellie patted her stomach. 'I haven't told many people yet, but I'm having another Christmas baby. This one's due just after Mae's second birthday.'

'That's amazing, congratulations.' Georgia hugged Ellie, fighting off the pang of envy that stuck in her throat. If things had been different, she was certain she'd have wanted children of her own, but the jealousy wasn't about that, it was about all the things her mother would never have. Caroline would never get to watch Georgia get married, or hold her grandchild in her arms. It was stupid to feel guilty when the whole thing was out of her hands, but she couldn't help it.

'I might be in trouble with Freya, because I'm supposed to be her maid of honour in December.'

'Surely she won't mind you being pregnant?' Georgia said, as Ellie followed her through the open bi-fold doors into the cabin. It was nice to talk about the everyday sort of problems that other people had, and Georgia liked Ellie all the more for not treating her differently. Conversations like this made her feel normal, even if it was only for an hour or two, before the next text popped up on her phone, reminding her of an upcoming hospital visit or appointment.

'No, as you saw when she helped with Cliffview, Freya's lovely. When she discovered, after her mum died, that Alan was her real father, it was like getting the sister I always wanted. It's just my due date is so close to the wedding that I'm not sure if I'll even end up making it. Even if I do, I looked awful when I was pregnant with Mae. My head and my neck seemed to merge together as one big blob and I had melasma, which made my face go all blotchy. They call it the mask of pregnancy and I could have done with a mask! I looked like Jabba the Hutt. I'm just not sure I want all of that captured for posterity in Freya's wedding pictures, even if I'm not in labour on the big day.'

'None of that matters because you'll be making memories. Even if you did look as bad as you think, which I highly doubt, when you look back on it, it'll just make you all laugh.' Georgia switched the kettle on. 'I wish I could track down a long lost sister to fill my place when I'm gone. I hate the thought of Mum missing out on all of that, much more than I mind missing out on it myself.'

'Oh God, Georgia, I'm so sorry.' Ellie looked mortified. 'Here I am, whingeing on about nothing, when you've got real things to contend with.'

'You're not whingeing at all.' Georgia smiled. 'I like hearing about what life is like for a normal family.'

'I'd hardly call us normal!' Ellie tried to laugh, despite the glassy look in her eyes.

'Don't get upset, I'm not sad for myself. It's just that I want Mum to have all of that. Richard's got two sons at university, and he lost his wife a few years ago, so it's another reason I want things to work out for him and Mum. Those boys will probably have children one day, even if it's ten or fifteen years from now, and that might give Mum the chance to be a grandma after all. I know I can't wave a magic wand for her, but if One Wish could really grant the impossible, that's what I'd have wished for, even if it meant missing out on Cliffview.'

'Maybe we could do something to give your mum and Richard a helping hand?' Ellie had that same look of determination on her face that she'd had when she'd persuaded Georgia to take Cliffview for the summer. 'After all, Seabreeze Farm has got a reputation for weaving a magic all of its own when it comes to pulling off romantic grand gestures.'

'What have you got in mind?'

'Are there any special occasions coming up, when your mum could be persuaded to come here for a celebration?'

'Mum won't need any encouragement to come up here, especially if she thinks it'll give her a chance to check up on me.' Georgia laughed. 'But it's her birthday next week.'

'Perfect. How about dinner for her and Richard in the

gazebo? It's got an even better view of the sea than you've got from your veranda, and we could decorate it with all the things your mum loves. We'll plan a menu and some music around her favourite things too. That's got to give us a chance of creating an extra bit of romance between her and Richard, hasn't it? Do you think he'll be up for it?'

'I'm almost certain he will.' Georgia's mind was already working overtime. If she could get her mum and Richard to make enough good memories together over the summer, that had to bond them together when she was gone, didn't it?

'You've captured that look Gerald has perfectly. I'm never sure if he's about to nuzzle my shoulder for a treat or sink his big, piano key teeth into my arm when I see him!' Gabe looked over Georgia's shoulder at the sketchpad on the table, and she resisted the urge to cover it up so he couldn't examine her latest drawing in front of her. Part of being an artist was sharing her work and opening it up for criticism, but having someone literally leaning over her shoulder whilst they offered up the critique was a whole different thing.

'I keep imagining the things that are running through his head. The looks he gives me sometimes make me laugh and I'm sure I actually heard him sigh the other day, when some of the other donkeys were chasing each other around the field like the fools he clearly thinks they are. He can definitely roll his eyes!'

'Maybe we should write his story. It would be like Peabody and the Coconuts! Do you remember that?' Gabe was laughing as she turned to look at it him.

'Oh my God! Not until you just reminded me, but we were so into that story weren't we? I don't think I'd have got through that summer without it.' It was not long after they'd started secondary school. Gabe had torn a tendon trying, and failing, to impress his new friends with a sliding tackle on a makeshift football pitch in the park. Georgia had caught chicken pox from her four-year-old next-door neighbour, years after all of her school friends had already been through it and moved on. Combining the spots from the virus with adolescent bad skin, had left her face looking like a plate of baked beans on toast. So the last thing she'd wanted to do was go out. Gabe was largely stuck in the house too and, having already had chicken pox, there was nothing to keep the two of them apart. They'd both found solace in drawing, painting and taking photographs of everything they could get their hands on, during their enforced isolation, as well as in spending time with one another.

Georgia had discovered an uncanny ability to draw peapods with faces that made them look like people and Gabe had stuck googly eyes on all the coconuts his mother had stockpiled for running a stall at the upcoming church summer fayre. They'd ended up creating a storyboard made up of pictures Georgia had drawn and print outs from Gabe's digital camera, which was how the story of Peabody and the Coconuts was born. They'd come up with a series of adventures, although in truth it was mainly Gabe who'd written out the story, which always involved the apparently much more vulnerable Peabody ultimately saving the day for his outwardly tougher coconut friends. Once they'd recovered they agreed on pain of death to never, ever, show anybody the drawings or stories. Having just moved up to secondary school, the idea of anyone knowing they wrote such childlike stories was mortifying, worse than having to do PE in a pair of gym knickers or lost property shorts when you forgot your kit. So Peabody and the Coconuts had been consigned to history for the best part of twenty years, lost forever as far as Georgia had known.

'I'm pretty sure Mum's still got the storyboards in her loft.' Gabe had the decency to look sheepish, as Georgia's eyebrows shot up behind her fringe.

'You told me you'd chucked them out! In fact, I seem to recall you telling me, no, *promising* me, that you'd burnt them all on the bonfire your dad had when he took down that old shed in the back garden, that same summer.'

'I was going to, but then Mum peeled the eyes off the coconuts to get them ready for the fayre and I couldn't bring myself to burn the photos of them or the pictures of Peabody. I felt bad.' Gabe laughed again, clearly realising how ridiculous that sounded, coming from someone only a year off turning thirty. But, if Georgia was honest, she knew where he was coming from. The whole reason she'd given him the storyboards to get rid of was because she couldn't face ripping them up and throwing them in the bin either. They might have been pre-teens, trying to show the world and their peers, just how grown up they'd become, but deep down they were still the same uncool kids they'd always been. She'd happily have carried on writing and drawing Peabody and the Coconuts stories way beyond when her chicken pox had finally disappeared, if Gabe had suggested it. She couldn't confess that, though, not even to Gabe, so she'd left him to get rid of the evidence.

'I knew I wouldn't have been able to chuck them out, but I never guessed you'd be as sentimental!' Georgia laughed as he shrugged in response, and she had an almost overwhelming urge to lean into him and tell him another secret she'd kept hidden, for almost as long as he'd hidden the truth about Peabody and the Coconuts. But every time she plucked up the courage to think about telling him the truth, she remembered how much there was to lose.

'I know. I was so busy trying to be something I wasn't and acting tough back then, but I actually had tears in my eyes watching Mum peeling the googly eyes off Colin and Clive!'

'Do you really think your mum's kept the storyboards all this time?'

'Knowing her, it's almost guaranteed. I've got to go round there later, so I'll go and have a look if you like?'

'That would be brilliant.' Georgia didn't want to get too hopeful, just in case they had ended up in a wheelie bin during a clear out of Gabe's parents' loft over the years. 'It'll be a laugh to see how awful they are, although I really thought we were creating a masterpiece back then.'

'Your drawings won't be rubbish, they never were. Not even back in nursery.' Gabe kissed her forehead and her skin tingled all the way down to her toes. 'I've got to meet up with a client in town and then I'll go to Mum and Dad's. I'll be back in time to drive you to dialysis though.'

'Thanks, see you later.' Watching Gabe disappear, Georgia touched the place on her forehead where he'd kissed her, trying to work out if she'd have had the guts to tell him how she felt if she hadn't been dying. Probably not, but she had to take any upside she could get from being told her days were numbered. It gave her an excuse to keep her feelings for Gabe hidden and, unlike the storyboards for Peabody and the Coconuts, she had absolutely no intention of dragging them out of the darkness.

* * *

Caroline felt seriously overdressed for a meal in Gerry's and it wasn't quite what she'd been expecting when Richard had told her he was taking her somewhere special to celebrate her birthday. The diet she'd been trying hard to stick to was starting to pay off and she was wearing a size-sixteen dress that she hadn't managed to zip up for at least a couple of years. It was long and floaty, the sort of thing Caroline imagined she might wear if she were ever invited to a garden party. Not that she moved in those sorts of circles.

Maybe Gerry's wasn't an up market restaurant, but it was still a really special place to her and she could understand Richard picking it. The tearoom, along with the rest of Seabreeze Farm, was so tied up with all the good memories she'd made with Georgia since her health had started to really deteriorate, and the farm had been a special place to them for years before that. So a birthday dinner in Gerry's was about as close to perfect as Richard could have made things, even if she did wish she'd kept her outfit a bit more casual.

'Karen's reserved what she says is your usual table?' Richard opened the door to the tearoom and smiled. He had such an open, friendly face and it was the first thing that had attracted Caroline to his profile, when Georgia had all but held her in an arm lock and forced her to sign up to the dating website. Like her, Richard had been widowed, and unlike a few of the other men she'd chatted to online, he hadn't asked her any questions about sex, or worse still, sent her a picture of his anatomy.

Even Georgia had been shocked by some of the messages Caroline had received. She'd said she might have expected it from a dating app like Tinder, but the website where Caroline had met Richard had been specifically set up for widows and widowers over the age of fifty, seeking a second chance at love. It turned out that didn't weed out the weirdos, although there were probably just as many propping up the bar in her local pub. Still, Caroline felt incredibly lucky to have found someone like Richard without having to go on a string of disastrous dates. The trouble was, her inner voice kept nagging at her: *if things seem too good to be true, then they probably are.* She was so used to getting bad news over the years, with all of Georgia's health conditions, she'd stopped expecting things to go well a long time ago.

Richard's two sons had come back home for the Easter holidays and Caroline had braced herself for things changing once they were back. She was worried that the boys might not like her, or maybe Richard's free time would be filled again, spending it all with his sons, and he wouldn't want to spend time with Caroline. But her fears had been unfounded. Richard had cooked dinner for her and the boys and they'd got on brilliantly. The boys seemed really interested in Caroline and asked her lots of questions, but it was clear they had their own lives and lots of plans for the summer, when they'd next be home, as well as both having already lined up jobs. Richard had phoned her after she'd got home, to tell her how much the boys had enjoyed meeting her. Jamie, his younger son, had apparently told Richard to make sure he held on to Caroline, as he'd found himself a good one. His older son, Dan, had confided he'd been worried about how Richard would cope when the boys finally moved out for good, especially as he had plans to go travelling with his girlfriend once his master's degree was awarded. Dan had said that his dad meeting Caroline had been like a weight being lifted.

If Caroline hadn't known better, she'd have been suspicious that Georgia had been working on Jamie and Dan, and that the three of them were in cahoots together to fast track things between her and Richard. Either way, it was nice to know that the boys approved, even if the two of them and Georgia were getting way ahead of themselves. Richard was great, but the truth was they were still getting to know each other and, no matter how much their kids might not want to hear it, they were years away from making the sort of commitment Georgia was pushing for. She had no fear that Richard might suddenly drop to one knee and pop the question.

'If I had to be stuck in one place forever, I couldn't think of many places I'd rather be than in this spot.' Caroline took a seat at the table where she and Georgia always sat. It was light until around 9 p.m. at this time of year and there was still a clear view down to the field where Gerald and the others were enjoying some evening sun.

'Happy birthday!' Karen suddenly appeared from behind Richard carrying a tray with a single cupcake in the middle and a couple of glasses of something fizzy.

'Thank you so much.' Caroline gave Karen a hug once she'd set the tray down on the table.

'I know a single cupcake isn't much, but I don't want to spoil Richard's dinner plans.' Karen exchanged a look with Richard, but Caroline was still none the wiser about what was going on. 'Georgia told me that red velvet was your favourite and of course everyone loves champagne, don't they?'

'I think I could manage a glass!' The cupcake was piled high with an expertly swirled layer of icing, so perfect that it almost didn't look real. There was a solitary candle in the middle, which hadn't been lit. But if Caroline did get the chance to blow a candle out, there was only one wish she wanted to make and, despite the promise she'd made to herself not to think about it for at least one night, she couldn't help it. 'Maybe you should get a picture of me blowing out the candle on the cupcake and put it on your Instagram page. I think everyone would be able to guess what I'm wishing for.'

'Great idea. I've had loads of people commenting that they've signed up to be matched as live donors or joined the organ donor register. I'm sure it won't be long before they find someone who can help Georgia out, but I know that's only half the battle.' Karen put a hand on her shoulder and Caroline wasn't sure she trusted herself to speak. Even half the battle would be a massive step in the right direction, but she couldn't let herself contemplate the alternative for too long, or she'd go mad. 'Let's light the candle and get this wish out there. Richard, are you okay to get a picture of Caroline? Ellie tells me I can't be trusted!'

'Absolutely. I'll video it and then I can screen shot the perfect image.'

'Nobody likes a show off!' Caroline gave him a gentle nudge and she leant forward as Karen lit the candle. There was no point in her keeping this wish a secret, as anyone who knew her would know exactly what she was wishing for anyway. 'Please let Georgia find a donor.' There was nothing else she wanted and she'd give up everything to make it happen, if she could.

'How have you enjoyed your birthday?' Georgia turned to her mother and smiled, as they sat under the gazebo which had uninterrupted views across the Channel towards the twinkling lights of the French coast on the other side. The darkness had cloaked both sides of the Channel and it was possible that someone sitting outside, enjoying a summer evening in France, was looking over at the lights strung across the gazebo on Seabreeze Farm.

'It's been great, thank you darling.' Caroline squeezed her hand. 'It's been all the things I love best. A bit of romance, fabulous food, good friends, but most of all, you.'

'Well I am a complete prize!' Georgia grinned. 'You can go and join in with the game if you want. I'm happy here, just watching everyone and looking at the view. You'd think I'd get bored with that now that I'm living at Cliffview, but I honestly don't think I ever could.'

'Playing rounders in the dark is bound to end in disaster, even if they are using a fluorescent softball.' Caroline topped up their glasses, the only difference being that Georgia's was alcohol free. It was boring, but there were a thousand things she missed more than a glass of wine, things she wouldn't even have given a second thought to before. Even the stuff she'd probably have moaned about, like getting up for work on a Monday morning.

'Just get ready to catch a rogue ball if it comes in this direction, so you don't lose your champagne. I think Richard's the one to watch; he's already sent a ball sailing over the cliffs.'

'He played cricket for the county youth team, back when he was at school. And one of his sons, Jamie, is in the county under-twenty-ones squad. I think he's what you call a ringer.'

'No wonder Alan wanted him on his team!' Georgia turned again as there was a cheer from the paddock just beyond them. 'Looks like Gabe's caught Richard out, so you can get back to your romantic evening now.'

'I think I've had all the romance I can take for the next decade; I'm not used to it. I thought we were just going to have dinner in Gerry's when he took me in there, but then to come out here and have dinner served under the stars... It was amazing.' Even in the half light, Georgia could have sworn she saw her mum's cheeks flush with colour. 'It probably sounds cheesy to you, but walking up the pathway lined with lanterns and seeing all the bowls of floating candles and flowers on the table, it was like something out of a movie.'

'He chose the right things then?'

'I'm guessing he had more than a little help?'

'I suggested one or two things, but some of this was definitely his own work. He's a really good guy, Mum. Don't forget that, whatever happens, will you? Promise me.'

'He's lovely, but I don't want to make any promises I might not be able to keep. He might get fed up with me first.'

'I doubt that, not judging by the way he looks at you. Even if it is a bit difficult to watch your mum getting all mushy with someone. Especially for someone like me, who finds romantic gestures about as comfortable as root canal surgery.'

'I think it's just the grand gestures you don't like, you know, the sort of things that happen at the end of a rom com. But romance comes in different forms. Richard knows I love the Cornish pasties from Dunn's bakery, but unless I get into town by about 10 a.m. they've always sold out. Last Saturday, when he popped to the barbers to get his hair cut before he had to drive Jamie up to Birmingham for a job interview, he took the time to pick me up a Cornish pasty and drop it off, so I could enjoy it with a cup of tea for lunch. It might sound like nothing to anyone else, but it meant a lot to me. It made me realise that not only does he listen, but he's thinking about me and making me a priority even when I'm not there. Tonight was brilliant, but that's *real* romance.'

'I suppose you're right. Although I couldn't tell you what I think romance looks like if my life depended on it.' Georgia shrugged. They both knew she hadn't had a romantic relationship for years and even when she'd dated, in school and at uni, she'd never been in love. Not unless the idea of love depicted in every book or movie she'd ever seen was a big fat lie. She might have been able to believe that, if her heart wasn't still doing a weird little skip every time Gabe looked in her direction. It was bloody inconvenient, but she loved him and it was getting much worse since they'd started living together. There was nothing she could do about it, except keep pretending it wasn't happening.

8

It was Georgia's birthday a week after her mum's, but she had no plans to make a big deal out of it and she'd forbidden her mum or Gabe from telling Ellie or Karen about it. Karen was delivering dialysis-friendly treats every other day as it was, and Georgia had struggled to get the zip done up on her jeans the morning before her birthday. She'd lost so much weight since starting the dialysis diet, so it was a shock to discover she could still go in the other direction with a constant supply of Karen's cooking motivating her to eat far too much. There wasn't much she could do in the way of physical exercise either. It was far more tempting just to sit and look out at the view, or wander very slowly down to see Gerald and his friends, which was about as athletic as she got these days.

Caroline and Richard had come up to see her on the morning of her birthday and taken her down into Kelsea Bay, where she'd picked up some seafood and moules marinière from a stall on the harbour. Gabe had insisted he was cooking dinner and Karen had dropped off another batch of the brownies she'd made the day before, so they'd be able to recreate the last visit they'd had to Bruges. Although, if Gabe's usual cooking disasters were anything to go by, they could end up with food poisoning instead. That trip was the closest their relationship had ever come to crossing the line into something else and it had been the only time Georgia had really wondered if Gabe felt more than friendship for her too. They'd been walking around the town, gazing up at the buildings that looked as if they should be encased inside snow globes, when the atmosphere between them had suddenly seemed to change.

'We should come back here at Christmas, I bet it's even more beautiful then.' Georgia had turned towards Gabe as she spoke, and he'd looked at her for what felt like an eternity before he answered.

'I'd like that, but I don't want the fact that you spend so much time with me to spoil your chances of meeting someone else.'

'I could say the same about you.'

'I can put it down to wanting to keep my freedom. You know me, I've always been a player!' He was already laughing by the time he got to the last word and she couldn't help joining in. Gabe was anything but a player, even though he could have been if he wanted to be. He was slim, but with the broad chest and shoulders of a rugby player. He'd been told a few times that he reminded people of Freddie Flintoff. After he'd mentioned it once too often, Georgia had threatened to get a T-shirt made with *I look a tiny bit like Freddie Flintoff* emblazoned across the front. If she'd been forced under thumbscrew torture to tell the truth, she'd have had to admit she didn't think Freddie was a patch on Gabe.

'Oh and I suppose a woman can't be a player?' When she'd finally managed to stop laughing, she'd attempted to give him a level look.

'You could give it a go, but I think a spinster of this parish might be closer to the mark.' He laughed again and as she'd pretended to push him away, their hands brushing together. She'd gone through a phase of reading Regency romances, at about the same time as she was studying history GCSE, trying to convince herself that it counted as revision. Almost all the romances she'd read described a touch between two people that lit up every nerve ending in their bodies, but she'd never felt anything like it – until then.

Looking at Gabe in that moment, she could have convinced herself he felt it too. For a split second she'd allowed her body to move forward, to lean slightly closer in to his. If he'd mirrored her, they'd have been close enough to kiss. But Gabe hadn't moved and she'd pulled back as though she'd been burnt, silently cursing herself for being so stupid and nearly doing something that would have embarrassed them both. Since then she'd kept her feelings buried all the deeper, and if things had ever had a chance of changing between her and Gabe it would have been up to him to make the first move. But he never had and so here they still were: friends to the end. It was something else she might have mourned – the fact that she'd die without ever being loved the way she loved Gabe – if their relationship hadn't already been one of the greatest gifts of her life.

'Dinner will be about ten minutes,' Gabe called out just as Georgia was finishing up her latest drawing of Holly, the lame sheep that Ellie had rescued from a local farm, after she'd been destined for the abattoir because only three of her legs worked properly. It was a good job Georgia wasn't a sheep, or she'd have been sent for the chop a long time back.

Gabe had brought the storyboards for Peabody and the Coconuts back from his parents' house and, in the evenings, he'd started to write a new story to go with the pictures that Georgia was drawing of the farm. She'd put a few of them on her blog, and Ellie had shared them to the social media accounts for the farm and Gerry's tearoom. They'd already had loads of messages asking for more.

Staying in and working on the story every night was like being those twelve-year-old kids in isolation all over again, and sometimes the world felt as if it didn't extend beyond Cliffview. One day, when Georgia was no longer around, Gabe would meet someone who'd force him out of his comfort zone and make him want to commit to a relationship. When that time came, she had no doubt that Gabe would eventually make a fantastic father, too, and leaving behind the story they'd created together would make her a tiny part of that. She could cry or punch a wall because she'd never get the chance to be a much bigger part of that, the way she wanted to, but she chose to focus on the part she could play in Gabe's future instead. It was the reason driving her to paint and draw more and more. Plus the fact that the sales of the merchandise featuring Gerald and his friends had already raised hundreds of pounds for One Wish.

'Can I give you a hand with anything?' Georgia looked up when Gabe came outside after the promised ten minutes. She couldn't smell burning, which was a promising start.

'No, just clear a space and I'll bring the food out. Do you want me to take the pictures in?' Gabe waited as she stacked everything into a pile on a tray, the latest watercolour drying on the top.

'I love this one. It looks like Holly's plotting to take over the world.'

'I can't wait to read the storyline you come up with to go with it.' Their hands touched as Georgia handed him the tray and that same feeling she'd had in Bruges hit her all over again.

'Dinner first and then I've got you a couple of presents.' He shook his head before she had a chance to respond. 'Don't even bother asking what they are, because I've kept them a secret for this long, so I'm definitely not going to tell you now.'

'Spoilsport.' She stuck out her tongue as he disappeared back into the kitchen. They might never have been more than friends, but if she'd had to make a list of all the things she was thankful for, she'd have put having Gabe in her life right at the top.

'That was lovely.' Georgia pushed the dessert plate away from her and sat back in her chair, wondering if Gabe would judge her if she undid the top button on her jeans, the waistband of which was cutting into her flesh. It was only Gabe, though, and he'd seen far worse over the years, especially dealing with the fall out of her illness; everything from injection sites, to comforting her whilst she thrashed around with the stomach cramps that were often a side effect of her dialysis. Seeing her stomach spilling over the top of her unbuttoned jeans would be nothing for Gabe.

'It's present time now then.' Gabe pulled a large gift box out from under the table and cleared a space in front of her, before setting it down. 'This is gift number one, but you need to read what's on the piece of paper inside before it'll make sense.'

'Okay.' Georgia untied the ribbon and lifted the lid off the box. She could already see two piles of DVDs under the piece of yellowing lined paper lying face down on the top. Turning the piece of paper over, she found a list with two columns, which she'd forgotten had ever existed.

'Do you remember when we made this?' Gabe's voice was gentle and she had to fight to stop the tears that were already threatening to spill out.

'I do.' They'd been about to turn eighteen and having to decide whether to go straight on to university from art college, or take a year out to go travelling. Georgia's diabetes had become more and more difficult to control and so they'd agreed to defer the travelling until they finished university, by which time they'd convinced themselves that Georgia's diabetes would be well under control and she'd be free to travel wherever she wanted to go.

Instead of planning their trip, they'd made a list of all the places they wanted to go when they finally got to travel and they'd listed them in two separate columns under their names. Gabe had always been a bit more adventurous than her, and trekking through the rainforest was top of his list. He'd have been happy to spend his travelling time living in hostels and camping out rough, whereas she preferred the idea of staying in hotels, so they'd probably never have been the right match as one another's travel companions, even if they'd got the chance. Her list of destinations could have been crossed off as a decade's worth of summer holidays, but in the end they'd never even got to do that.

By the time they'd finished university, any chance of travelling much further than the other side of the Channel, where she could get back home in an hour or two if she needed to, was over. And it wasn't long before even that was impossible. She'd told Gabe more than once that he should go travelling anyway, but he insisted that he'd gone off the idea and wanted to concentrate on growing his career. It was obvious it had been about protecting her so she didn't feel she was missing out and it was just one more reason why she loved him so much, even if she did feel guilty that he'd missed out too.

The list was a representation of the life they'd never had the chance to live and all the places they'd never got to see. It wasn't not being able to go and stand on the top of the Empire State Building or stare up at the ceiling of the Sistine Chapel that broke her heart. After all, she could almost be there in the countless Instagram reels that made living vicariously through someone else's experiences a possibility. What she missed the most about never getting the chance to take those trips was sharing them with Gabe, holding his hand as they strolled through a piazza, or watching his face as he saw the places he'd longed to travel to for the very first time. She'd trade a trip around the world for another day with Gabe every single time.

'I found the list in the same pile of stuff the storyboards were in. I know it's old school but, because you haven't had a chance to visit most of the places on your list yet, I found a film set in each of the locations and ordered the DVDs for each of them. I've added the ones I could find on Netflix to your list on there too.'

'That's amazing.' Georgia couldn't look at him, because if she did, he'd see the truth written all over her face. He knew her better than anyone, after all. There wasn't another person in the world who'd do this for her and understand why it was so important. Which meant he'd also be able to see the effect he'd had on her, if he looked her in the eye, and she was terrified he'd see the rest too and know just how deeply and utterly in love with him she was. So instead, she flicked through the first few DVDs, forcing herself to concentrate on the covers and never once making eye contact with Gabe. There was *Only You*, set in Rome, *You've Got Mail*, in New York, *Fifty First Dates*, set in

Hawaii, and *Out of Africa*. They were all the places she'd chosen on her side of the list and they had something else in common too. 'They're all romances. Did you realise that?'

'Are they?' Gabe kept his tone even and when she finally forced herself to look at him, she was relieved to see him smiling. Maybe there was a chance she could make a joke of this too and keep her feelings hidden away where they belonged. But Gabe got in first. 'I suppose it's because most of the places on your list would be classed as romantic too. Who'd have thought it!'

'I can be romantic.' She grinned at the look on his face, thankful that the moment when she'd thought all her vulnerabilities might be exposed had passed. 'Oh all right, maybe not, but I'm looking forward to watching these and finally having a clue.'

'There's something else, but I'll be a couple of minutes because I've left it over with Ellie at the main house. While I'm gone, do you want to choose a film for us to watch, to start your romantic education?'

'Okay, see you in a bit.' It was funny how quickly she'd got used to him being around all the time and if anyone else had told her that she could miss someone who was only gone for ten minutes, she'd have laughed, or pretending to gag. But it was just another inconvenient truth she was learning to live and die with. Distracting herself, she went back through the DVDs and, by the time she heard Gabe coming back down the path to Cliffview, Georgia had chosen *Before Midnight*, a film set in Greece that she'd never seen before.

'Are you ready for your second present?' Gabe's voice drifted in from outside through the open bi-fold doors.

'I am, but you've got me more than enough presents already.' She didn't think she could take one more thoughtful gesture and hold on to the secret she was desperately trying to hide from Gabe. If he carried on like this, he was bound to find out, even if she never said the words out loud.

'Okay here we go.' Gabe came into the cabin with what looked like a bundled up blanket in his arms. As he pulled the top of the blanket back, Georgia's second present was finally revealed. A little black pug was staring back at her, and it was obvious from first glance that it only had one eye. 'This is Ruby. She's not a raving beauty admittedly, but the breeder she came from sent her to an animal shelter to be re-homed. She had to have her eye removed when she was only two months old. Someone from the shelter is friends with Ben and they asked him if he knew anyone who might want her. She's got a bit of a problem with one of her back legs being a tiny bit shorter than the other one too. But when Ben told me about her, and I went to see her, I thought she was perfectly imperfect and I had a funny feeling you would too.'

'Can we really keep her?' Georgia was already on her feet and ten seconds later Ruby was in her arms, nuzzling her neck. This time she didn't even try to hide her emotions and tears were rolling down her cheeks into the little dog's fur.

'Yep, she's ours. There's no getting away from me now.' Gabe rubbed the dog's head and Georgia felt a huge wave of love wash over her, for him and for the little pug sandwiched between them. She was never going to be a mother, but it didn't matter. She had Gabe and now she had Ruby. That was more than enough for her, for however long it lasted.

* * *

Someone was using a chainsaw to chop down trees at God knows what time in the morning, there couldn't be any other explanation for it. Except that when Georgia opened her eyes, an alternative explanation suddenly presented itself. Ruby was lying on the bed beside her, flat on her back, with her legs in the air, snoring at a volume that Georgia wouldn't have believed possible if she hadn't heard it for herself.

'George, are you awake?' Gabe knocked on the door as he spoke, and Ruby flipped a complete one-eighty straight on to her feet. Her one eye blinked as she tried to make sense of where she was, before launching herself towards Georgia's head and giving her a slobbery kiss.

'If I wasn't already awake, I would be now with a pug for an alarm clock! Come in.' Georgia fought to disentangle herself from the dog, who was now burrowing under the duvet. 'No need for a shower either this morning, now that Ruby's given my face a wash with her tongue!'

'I could hear her snoring from next door. At least I assume it was Ruby?' Gabe grinned, jumping out of the way as she threw a pillow at him.

'I honestly thought someone was sawing up wood when I first heard her this morning.'

'Are you starting to have second thoughts about letting her sleep on the end of your bed?'

'I'd rather put up with snoring than hear her crying, but I might have to start having an afternoon nap if this keeps up. I had no idea that having a dog would give me a real taste of what it must be like to have a baby, but she woke me up at least three times last night.' Georgia yawned, stretching her arms out as she did, the duvet slipping down slightly until she grabbed it and pulled it up around her neck. Not that Gabe was fazed.

'Don't worry, I've seen it all before. I'll go and organise some tea and toast, if you're ready for a bit of breakfast? Just put on some clothes first, can you? And save us all!' Gabe laughed, but he was too quick for her and out of the room before she had a chance to hurl another pillow at him. He was perfectly safe anyway; she was wearing a nightdress, even if it had been in danger of revealing a lot more than she wanted it to.

'Nice pyjamas.' Gabe was setting the coffee pot on the table as Georgia came through the open bi-fold doors, with Ruby so close on her heels that she had to be careful not to tread on her.

'They're my Christmas ones. I'm not sure how they ended up in my suitcase, but I want to have a shower before I get dressed and I didn't want to risk subjecting you to a flash of flesh again.' Georgia raised her eyebrows. It was a relief to be back to joking with Gabe, after how close she'd come to letting her emotions spill over on her birthday. The morning was ushering in another glorious day on the Kent coast and she could already feel the warmth of the sun on the deck under her bare feet.

'Red always suited you.' Gabe looked at her as if he really meant it. 'What do you want on your toast?'

'You don't have to wait on me.'

'It's fine. I'm not working today, so I need an excuse to have a leisurely breakfast on the veranda and, if I'm making you breakfast, at least no-one can accuse me of being lazy.'

'I don't think anyone could do that.' Georgia pulled out one of the chairs. Not only had Gabe been working on his normal contracts and commissions, but he'd also been auctioning off shoots to raise money for One Wish. And he'd worked as hard as anyone to help finish Cliffview as quickly as possible. Ellie had also told her that he'd offered to help out on the farm if they needed him, as a way of saying thank you for all they'd done. So it probably did feel like a treat for Gabe to sit down, enjoy the view, and have a piece of toast without interruption.

'Marmite then? Just a thin scraping of course.'

'You know me too well.'

'I'd hope so by now.' Gabe gestured towards the table in front of her. 'I brought your phone out. It was charging in the kitchen, but it rang three times while I was making the tea and I thought it might be something important.'

'You don't think it's the shelter, do you?' Georgia had been paranoid about the animal shelter that had re-homed Ruby ringing up and saying there'd been some terrible mistake, and that she wasn't going to be allowed to keep the little dog after all. She couldn't help thinking that no-one in their right mind would re-home a dog with someone who was dying, even if Gabe had agreed to continue looking after Ruby when she was no longer there. But Gabe was already shaking his head.

'No-one's going to take Ruby away from you, I've promised you that. Just see if you recognise the number; it's probably nothing.'

Georgia picked up the phone. There were two missed calls from the same number and when she pasted it into google, it came up as the number for a children's publishers in London. It had to be a wrong number, but the voice mail message icon was flashing.

'Hi this is Cassie James, one of the commissioning editors from Fiaba Books. One of my team found your illustrated stories about Seabreeze Farm from a link on the One Wish website, and their CEO passed on your contact details. I wondered if you could give me a call on this number, please, to discuss us buying the rights to publish it? We've been looking for something that might rival *The Boy, the Mole, the Fox and the Horse*, which you probably know has been a huge success. We really think your Seabreeze Farm stories could have the same appeal. Sorry to have rung you so early, but I'd like to talk to you before anyone else does. I look forward to hearing from you soon.'

Georgia had replayed the voicemail three times by the time Gabe brought two plates of toast to the table.

'Are you okay? You look a bit shell shocked...'

'I haven't lost the plot, have I? It's not 1 April, is it?'

'No, it's 11 May. Why?'

'I would have sworn this was an April Fools' Day joke, but apparently not. They want to publish our stories.' As Georgia said the words out loud they still wouldn't sink in.

'What stories? Peabody and the Coconuts?' Gabe screwed his face up; it clearly didn't make any sense to him either.

'No, the Seabreeze Farm stories we've been putting on the blog. That was one of the commissioning editors from Fiaba Books; they found our stories from a link on the One Wish website and they want to talk to us.' Georgia looked at her phone and it wouldn't have surprised her if it had suddenly shape-shifted into a unicorn. 'Do you think it's all a wind up?'

'Why would anyone do that? Your drawings are brilliant and it doesn't surprise me that someone wants to turn them into a children's book.'

'Your stories are what brought them to life and, if this is real, they want those as well as my illustrations. They even compared it to that book by Charlie Mackesy, the one everyone's saying is the new *Winnie the Pooh*.' Georgia shook her head again. This couldn't be real.

'We've always made a good team and this is great. The more people you can share your drawings with the better and think how much money this could raise for One Wish.' Gabe went to kiss her, just as she moved her head. He must've been aiming for her cheek, like he had thousands of times before. But instead their lips met and she was suddenly kissing him in a way that went way beyond friendship, and he was kissing her back. By the time she finally pulled away, she could barely breathe, let alone speak.

'I'm sorry.' Gabe looked horribly uncomfortable and she couldn't bear hearing him say it had all been a mistake, when it was already so obvious.

'Don't worry, it was a heat of the moment thing. You know, dreams coming true and having the chance to leave something behind. Who wouldn't want to kiss someone, anyone old someone who just happens to be around, when getting news like that?' She forced a smile and ten seconds later it was as though it had never happened. If it hadn't meant anything to Gabe, she couldn't let him know that it had meant something to her.

9

Since converting the farm into a wedding and events venue, there had been some parties with spectacular décor, but the way the barn had been decorated for the One Wish fundraising ball probably topped them all. There were thousands and thousands of white lights strung around the beams, not just from Seabreeze Farm's own supply, but from other venues that hosted One Wish events, which made it look breath-taking. There were also strings of bunting, made from white hessian, hung between the main beams, the flags delicately embroidered with all the names of the people who One Wish had helped since its launch. On each table was a large potted rose, donated by a local garden centre. After the event, all of the bushes would be planted in a new rose garden that One Wish would be creating at the hospice in Elverham. They were also going to add to the bunting with each new wish granted, putting it up at every big celebration the charity had from now on, so that no-one they'd helped would ever be forgotten, no matter what.

As lavish as the event looked, it was all down to the

generosity of the companies sharing or donating their resources, along with the work of volunteers. And not a penny of the money donated to One Wish to help make people's dreams come true had been spent on the ball. They'd set a target to raise at least £10,000 from the ball, from ticket sales, donations and an auction. Some of the auction items had been offered online too and the most popular had been the chance to have a family member or friend featured in one of the illustrations Georgia did of the animals. Gabe had also agreed to take photos at the ball and people would have the chance to buy prints, in exchange for a donation to the charity. All of which meant that Ellie was as confident as she could be that they'd reach the fundraising target, but she still had what felt like a swarm of butterflies fluttering against her ribcage. Letting down the team at One Wish wasn't an option.

'It looks fantastic in here.' Georgia got up from the wheelchair that Gabe had pushed into the barn. 'I'm glad we got in before it started, as every time I get out of this thing it makes me feel like I'm Andy from *Little Britain*, but if I'd walked from Cliffview, I might have had to lie on the dance floor for twenty minutes to recover.'

'You wouldn't have wanted to ruin those beautiful shoes either. You look amazing by the way.' Ellie kissed Georgia on both cheeks. She really did look fantastic and not just because the outfit and towering high heels she was wearing wouldn't have looked out of place on the cover of a glossy magazine. It was because Georgia looked so much healthier than she had when Ellie had first met her. It had been a beautiful spring, and summer seemed set to follow suit, which meant Georgia had a golden brown tan from having spent so much time outside. If Ellie hadn't known better, she'd have found it almost impossible to believe that Georgia was as seriously ill as she was.

'You look great too, and I've got to say, Ben and Alan scrub up well. There's definitely something about a man in a tuxedo.' Georgia grinned. 'Even Gabe looks pretty good.'

'Wow, no need to be so gushing.' Gabe laughed too and turned to Ellie. 'Although it might be the nicest thing George has ever said to me. So I probably need to hang on to it.'

'Well I think you look great, very James Bond. Actually, you'd pass for a young Daniel Craig I reckon.' Ellie barely finished the sentence before Georgia started to laugh.

'Oh no, he was bad enough after a couple of people told him he looked a bit like Freddie Flintoff. He's never going to let this one go.' Georgia might not be lavish with the compliments when it came to Gabe, but the more time Ellie had spent with the two of them, the more she'd come to realise that Georgia wasn't being honest with herself, let alone Gabe. Just the way she looked at him had been a dead giveaway and Ellie would have bet a month's turnover from the farm that Gabe felt exactly the same way. She didn't know either of them well enough to broach the subject and, even if she had, she could understand exactly why they might not want to admit how they felt to one another. Even without the complication of Georgia's prognosis, they had almost thirty years of friendship to put on the line.

'To be fair, Georgia's right, I might have to quote you and get that printed on my business cards.' Gabe laughed again. 'Where do you want me to set up?'

'Ben's organised everything for you over by the ice sculpture. He thought that would make a good backdrop and, if people share the photos on social media, it'll be a bit more advertising for the charity.' Ellie was impressed that Ben had managed to add a filter that popped up with the Seabreeze Farm location check-in, so people could add the One Wish logo to any selfies they took. The marketing side of things since starting the business had been a steep learning curve for them all, but it was brilliant to use what they'd learned to help out the charity.

'Okay great, thanks. I'll see you both later, but I've set myself a target to make the charity at least a thousand pounds tonight and I'm not stopping until I do.' Gabe gave Georgia a brief kiss on the cheek. 'Have a good time, but try not to nag your mum and Richard too much!'

'I'll try, but it's going to be difficult.' Georgia turned towards Ellie as Gabe walked away. 'He knows me too well sometimes. I keep hoping that Mum and Richard will make things a bit more permanent. I'm past hoping that they'll actually get married in time for me to be a bridesmaid, but I'd like to know for certain that this isn't just going to be a summer fling. Right now I'd settle for them booking a holiday together next summer, and Gabe knows I'll be nagging them to put a bid in for one of the holidays in the auction. I just want to know that Mum has things to look forward to when she doesn't have to worry about me any more. Her life has been on hold for far too long already.'

'I see lots of couples in this job and I'd bet good money that your mum and Richard have got what it takes to last.' Ellie swallowed the words that were threatening to bubble up in her throat. It would have been so easy to say that Georgia and Gabe had what it took too, but it was complicated. She'd also resisted the urge to brush off Georgia's comments about not being around, because in the short time she'd known her, she'd already realised how much Georgia hated anyone pretending everything was going to be okay.

'I hope you're right. It would make it so much easier for me to let go when the time comes.'

'There's still a chance you could have a transplant though, isn't there?' This time, Ellie couldn't stop the words spilling out.

'There's also a chance they'll ask Gabe to be the next James Bond, given his uncanny resemblance to Daniel Craig, and there's about the same odds of that happening. There are so many things I don't have any control over, it makes it tempting to try and control the things I might be able to influence, like making sure Mum's okay. I know I shouldn't be pushing as hard as I am, but I can't help it.'

'I get it. I was bad enough with Mum and Alan. When you've had a parent who's given you their all, you just want to see it paid back, don't you?'

'Exactly, and no-one deserves their chance at happiness more than Mum.'

'I'll be keeping everything crossed then.' Ellie glanced at her watch. 'I've put you on the same table as us, with your mum and Richard. I've just got to go and find Mum and check that she doesn't need my help with any last minute things before we get started. Will you be okay for a bit?'

'I'll be fine on my own and that way I can check out exactly which holidays I'm going to bid on for Mum and Richard. If it's a gift they can hardly say no, after all.' Georgia dropped a perfect wink and Ellie watched as she headed over to check out the list of auction lots. Maybe it was wrong of Georgia to try and orchestrate Caroline and Richard's relationship, but no-one could criticise her motivation. If Ellie could do anything to help, she would.

* * *

It had taken Georgia at least three attempts to persuade her mum and Richard to go and dance. Richard's excuse had been that he had two left feet and all the natural dancing ability of Teresa May, but Georgia knew the truth; they didn't want to leave her sitting on her own, like a teenager at a school disco who no-one was interested in. But if people watching had been an Olympic sport, Georgia would have reached gold medal standard years before and she was more than happy sitting on her own as a result. It was fascinating watching how people interacted when they didn't think anyone was looking. Ben was staying close to Ellie's side and he'd stopped her climbing on a chair to fix the end of one of the strands of bunting that had come loose. Anyone who watched them closely enough would have been able to guess the secret they were still holding close for now – that Ellie was pregnant. Karen and Alan laughed together almost constantly, but then Karen had a Ma Larkin sort of quality, which meant she was almost always smiling and it looked like she could burst into peals of laughter at any moment. Alan had a much less cheerful demeanour when he wasn't with Karen, but his whole face seemed to transform the moment he looked at her.

Now that her mum and Richard had finally taken to the dance floor, Georgia could watch them too. Caroline was leaning into him as he whispered in her ear, a slow smile spreading across her face. He'd been waiting on her all night too, getting her a drink if her glass was ever less than half full and standing up when she did, like a proper old-fashioned gent. Maybe some people would have called that sort of thing misguided, or even chauvinistic, but Caroline deserved to be fussed over. She'd spent nearly all her adult life caring for Georgia and putting her first, without anyone to lean on. This was her time and Richard was the right man for the job; Georgia was more certain of that than ever.

'I see you're indulging in your favourite pastime again. I

looked over earlier and I was clearly the focus of some of your people watching. So what's the verdict?' Gabe came up behind her and she turned to look at him. She couldn't possibly tell him the real verdict – that from watching him she'd realised he was the best person she knew. He put people at their ease and brought out the best in them, so he could capture a moment they'd treasure forever. Everybody warmed to Gabe and she'd seen three or four women desperately flirting with him, just during the time she'd been watching him. Not that he ever seemed to notice. Even if he had, he wouldn't have done anything about it and that was almost certainly because of her. He was prioritising her, just like he always had.

'Put it this way, I reckon you'll hit your fundraising target. I didn't see anyone turn down the chance of having their photograph taken.'

'I'm already over the target, thank goodness, as I'd hate to be the one to let the side down. I think I've successfully pressured everyone in the room into having their photos done, so I've come over to bother you now.' Gabe held out a hand. 'Fancy a dance?'

'I...' She didn't know what to say. They hadn't danced together in years, not since the end of uni ball when she'd caught her last serious boyfriend asking one of the waitresses for her phone number. He'd told her he was sorry, but that they were always going to end after uni anyway. It had been fun, but there was no way he wanted to be saddled on a long-term basis with the restrictions that Georgia's illness brought with it. Gabe had been at the ball with a group of friends from the university's rugby team, but he hadn't been part of a couple at the time. So when he'd seen Georgia go past, with tears already streaming down her face, he'd left the rest of his group and followed her outside the marquee. If it had been a rom com, the setting couldn't have been more romantic. There was a super moon, hanging so low in the sky that it didn't look real. The stars were also out in force and the night air was warm enough that she hadn't been shaking with cold, even in her strapless ball gown. The shaking had been down to emotion, but she couldn't tell whether it was anger or sadness.

Gabe hadn't tried to make it all okay and say the right things, when she'd told him what had happened. He'd known better than anyone that she hated platitudes and promises that everything would turn out fine. Instead, as the music had drifted out of the marquee, he'd taken hold of her hands and pulled her close to him. As he danced with her, she hadn't needed to be told it was all okay. She'd known it would be, as long as she had Gabe.

'Come on, I promise not to step on your toes. And it'll mean that your mum and Richard will stay on the dance floor for longer too, instead of thinking they need to come back and keep you company.' Gabe grinned, playing his trump card.

'You'd make a good blackmailer, do you know that?'

'I've got to get a dance somehow. I always seem to be a spare at things like this and, once again, I've ended up relying on you to dance with.' Gabe shrugged, taking hold of her hand as she finally stood up.

'In that case, I hope you realise how lucky you are to have me.' Georgia took his hand, hoping that deep down he understood what she was really saying.

'Oh, don't worry, I count my blessings every night! Come on then, let's show them how it's done.' Gabe led her on to the dance floor, just as the band began their rendition of 'Your Song' by Elton John. On the night of the uni ball, Gabe had held her close, but not close enough that anyone watching might have mistaken them for more than friends. But tonight he was pulling her closer still, until not even a piece of paper could have passed between them. He was just supporting her, that was all, holding her so close he was almost carrying her, taking the weight off her feet and the pressure off her rapidly failing heart.

It was the way a grown-up might have danced with a young child, except the feelings flooding Georgia's brain as she pressed up against Gabe were anything but innocent. The solid feel of his chest against hers, and the scent of his after shave as her head rested against his neck were doing something to her. She hoped to God that no-one was watching, the way she'd watched other people on the dancefloor, and judging her for taking advantage of Gabe when he had no idea what effect he was having on her body.

'You don't have to hold me so tight; I won't collapse on you.' Georgia forced herself to say the words that finally made Gabe loosen his grip.

'I'm sorry, it's just...' He paused for a moment, looking straight into her eyes. 'The other night, when we got the news from the publishers. The kiss.'

'I know, I know. It was a stupid, heat of the moment thing.' Georgia was determined to cut him off before he let her down gently. She couldn't bear to hear him say out loud that it had been a mistake, something he never wanted to repeat. 'I think we were both so shell shocked by the news we'd have kissed anyone!'

'George, I...' Gabe seemed to have developed a sudden inability to finish his sentences. 'I'm sorry.'

'For what?' Before he even had a chance to answer, the band switched to their next, much livelier, song and the dance floor started to fill with people. 'Shall we go and sit down?'

'I think that's a good idea. I've been a dad dancer since

long before it was a thing, and since I was way too young to be mistaken for anyone's dad. I'll be more than ready when the time comes!' It was a throwaway comment, but it knocked the air of Georgia's lungs all the same. It was times like this when she really wished she could knock back a couple of glasses of champagne from the bar, just to take the edge off the pain.

'You two looked very cosy out there; the perfect couple!' Karen was waiting back at the table when they arrived. 'Although I'm glad you've decided to come back; I couldn't remember if you'd had the chance to mee my stepdaughter, Freya, when she was down helping with the renovations at Cliffview?'

'We did meet really briefly, but it's lovely to see you again. Thanks so much for everything you did.' Georgia shook Freya's hand. She didn't look much like Alan, except when she smiled.

'It's lovely to see you again too and we really didn't do anything much with the renovations. We wanted to stay and help out for a lot longer, but I'd just taken on the role of matron at the hospital, so I could only take a week off and then, at the grand old age of thirty-two, Ollie got chicken pox!'

'It's supposed to be horrible when you get it as an adult. I got it when I was twelve and that was bad enough.' Georgia smiled. 'But it was lovely of you to help at all. Everyone has been amazing since your dad offered to let me stay at Cliffview. I could never thank them enough. I wish there was something I could do.'

'I think all the fundraising from your illustrations will probably more than pay them back and I hear you've even been offered a book deal?'

'That probably had more to do with Gabe's storytelling skills than my illustrations.'

'You know that's not true.' Gabe shook his head and Freya wasn't having any of it either.

'Definitely a team effort! And, like I say, you've done more than enough already, but I've got another favour to ask you.'

'Of course, if we can help, we will.' Georgia waited as Freya seemed to struggle to come out with it.

'It's a bit of an odd one, but I wanted to ask if you'd be my bridesmaid?'

'That's a lovely offer, but you really don't have to. I mentioned to Ellie ages ago about wanting to be a bridesmaid, but that was before I moved to the farm and got to witness so many weddings here.'

'Actually, you'd be helping me. Ellie wanted to back out completely, because she's worried about looking like Humpty Dumpty in the photos, but I've told her she's got to be there if she can. The trouble is, the baby's due the week after the wedding and there's no guarantee she'll even end up making it. The dress I'd already ordered for her would be a perfect fit for you, and it seems like such a shame for it not to be worn, but I don't want you to feel like you're just a reserve. I want you both there.' Freya's cheeks flushed with colour. 'And the truth is that ticking off another one of your dreams would make a great story to raise the profile of the book and the fundraising for One Wish.'

'So you're not just doing me a favour?' Georgia searched Freya's face, needing to be certain that she wasn't making the sacrifice of having a virtual stranger taking on a key role at her wedding, just to grant a dying girl's wish.

'Not at all. You'd be the one doing me a massive favour.'

'Right...' Georgia paused and she could have sworn that Karen and Freya were both holding their breath as they waited for her to answer. 'In that case, I'd be honoured and at least I can stop nagging poor old Richard to propose to Mum, just so I can finally get to walk down the aisle at Seabreeze Farm!'

'That's brilliant!' Karen and Freya spoke in unison, but as Georgia glanced at Gabe, his face seemed to fall. The same thing had probably crossed his mind that had crossed hers; she might not be up to walking anywhere – let alone being a bridesmaid – by the time December came around. But having something else to look forward to, especially once she'd moved out of Cliffview, could only be a good thing.

* * *

'You made me jump! I wasn't expecting to find anyone down here.' Ellie's heart was thudding in her ears as a rush of adrenaline shot through her body when Gabe stepped out of the shadows.

'Sorry. I just wanted to get some air, to try and get my head straight.' Even in the half light, Gabe looked like a tortured soul and Ellie felt tears stinging the backs of her eyes. This was about Georgia, she could tell just from looking at him.

'Do you want to talk about it?'

'I don't know if it will help, but I would like to talk it through with someone.' Gabe sighed. 'As long as I'm not keeping you?'

'I was just doing a quick check on the animals, to make sure they're going to be okay overnight.' Ellie wrapped the coat that she'd put on over her evening dress more tightly around her. 'I've got as long as you need.'

'I don't really know where to start, so I might as well just come out with it. I love Georgia.'

'I know you do.' Ellie reached out and touched his arm, wishing she knew him well enough to judge whether or not he'd appreciate a hug. But sometimes, when someone was only just holding it together, too much sympathy could push them over the edge.

'Not just in the way she thinks, the way best friends should love each other.' Gabe breathed out. 'I'm *in love* with her and, if I'm really honest, I can't remember a time when I haven't been.'

'Have you told her?'

'For years I've thought about whether or not it's the right thing to do and a couple of times I got really close to telling her, but there was always something stopping me. There never seemed to be a right moment, or if there was I let it pass me by, and now it's too late.'

'No, it isn't! You've got to tell her while you've still got the chance.'

'And what if she doesn't feel the same? What then? She'll pull away and I'll be pushed out of her life for however long we've got left. I couldn't cope with that.' Gabe shook his head. 'I couldn't stand missing out on a single moment when I could have been with her, just because I was too selfish to keep how I feel to myself.'

'I don't know either of you that well, but it's obvious she loves you too.'

'She loves me, but not in the way I love her. She's made it crystal clear that she doesn't. When the news came through from the publisher that they wanted to make our stories about the farm into a book, somehow we ended up kissing, but she couldn't wait to tell me it was nothing afterwards.'

'She's probably just as scared of being rejected as you are.' Ellie's voice was gentle. Gabe and Georgia were perfect together, but they were trapped in a stand-off, each one afraid to take the first shot. The trouble was, they didn't have forever to find the right moment. 'Please don't both make the same mistake and say nothing.'

'I was going to ask her to marry me tonight, after we got back from the ball.' Gabe shook his head. 'If she'd told me not to be ridiculous, I was going to pass it off as simply crossing one more thing off her list; just a way to grant her wish of being part of a Seabreeze Farm wedding. Promising to stay together until death do you part isn't the big deal to her that it is to other people. But I'd have been lying, pretending that was the reason I wanted to do it. The truth is, I'd give anything to be married to her for the next fifty or sixty years.'

'I think she'd want that too, if you told her the truth.'

'I can't risk it and I can't ask her to marry me now, because she's getting her Seabreeze Farm wedding already, as Freya's bridesmaid.'

'It's not the same thing.' Part of Ellie wanted to shout at him, to keep telling him over and over again until he got the message that he didn't need to worry because it was painfully obvious that Georgia loved him too. He just needed to tell her the truth. But she could understand how much he and Georgia thought they had to lose by being honest with one another. She'd given Gabe her opinion, because he'd asked for it, but now, as much as she didn't want to, she had to step back. Otherwise she'd be in danger of interfering in something that had nothing to do with her. If she did that and it backfired – making life even harder for Georgia and Gabe than it already was – she'd never be able to forgive herself.

10

———

At any moment, someone was going to tap Georgia on the shoulder and ask her what the hell she thought she was doing going to a wedding fayre, when she hadn't had a boyfriend in eight years and barely knew the bride-to-be whose coat tails she was riding on.

'I still feel like I shouldn't be here.' Georgia whispered the words to Ellie, who was sitting in between her and Freya, with Karen on the bride-to-be's other side.

'Don't be daft. I need all the help I can get to find a dress that won't make me look the shape of Mrs Potato Head.' Ellie was still going be maid of honour at the wedding, if she wasn't in labour, of course. She'd told Georgia a bit of background about Freya and Ollie's relationship, which had involved Freya's best friend trying to break the two of them up and had led Freya back to Seabreeze Farm. It had also led to the discovery that Alan was her real father and it had been rocky road for all of them for a little while. Looking at the family now, no-one would ever guess that they hadn't been a unit all along. Ellie had explained that being betrayed by her best friend had made

Freya extra cautious about choosing a bridesmaid and she didn't want to end up having a friend in her wedding photos who she fell out with later, or who just drifted away from her life at some point. It was why she'd originally only wanted Ellie and Mae. Georgia could have asked why she was less of a risk than anyone else, given that she barely knew Freya, but the answer was obvious, and the last thing she wanted was to make Ellie or Freya feel awkward when they'd both been so kind.

'Are we trying to find a particular colour?' Georgia looked up at the models coming down the catwalk in layers of tulle and satin. She had to admit that none of the dresses looked suitable for someone who was going to be nine months pregnant by the time the wedding came around.

'Your dress is sage green and Mae's got an ivory dress with a matching sage green waistband. So I think that's the colour Freya's looking for.' Ellie pulled a face. 'Maybe I should look in Argos for a toilet tent. They come in green, don't they?'

'You'll look great whatever you wear. Although they all seem to be wedding dresses so far.' Georgia would never admit it to anyone, but she'd known for years what sort of wedding dress she'd want if she ever got married. A classic Bardot-style dress that wouldn't look dated in ten years' time. Looking at her mum's wedding photos from the late eighties had made her cry with laughter as a teenager. Caroline's dress had huge puffy sleeves with a weird sort of concertina detail on the sides, like a half-open fan. There'd been white netting across the chest, a high lacy collar that was like a cross between a Tudor ruff and something out of a sci-fi movie. Not to mention loads of lace and rows of tiny pearls, with what looked like a scrunched up net curtain shoved under Caroline's tiara, which had more tiny pearl and diamanté droplets hanging down, like an overgrown fringe. It was hideous, there was no other word for it, even her mum thought so now. So it was classic and elegant all the way for Georgia.

Suddenly, there it was, on the model standing in front of her. It was such a simple dress – slightly off the shoulder with long sleeves, completely plain at the front and with a row of covered buttons going over half-way down the back. It was perfect and she found herself having to swallow hard to stop tears filling her eyes because she'd never have the chance to wear it. She'd never been the sort of person obsessed with getting married, although like most people she'd thought about it from time to time. It was only when she'd faced up to how quickly her version of forever would be over, that she'd realised just how much she'd wanted all of that with Gabe. Now here was the perfect dress, staring her in the face, but she didn't have forever and she didn't even really have Gabe.

'Now that's a lovely dress.' Ellie turned towards Georgia as she spoke.

'It's what I'd have chosen.' Georgia shook herself. She didn't want to end up like one of those women in a sit com, who had a wedding dress hanging in their wardrobe, without any hint of an occasion to wear it to. It was just one more dream that wasn't going to come true, no more important than any of the others. 'They're bringing out the bridesmaids dresses now; let's see if we can find you something slightly more flattering than a toilet tent.'

Twenty minutes later, Freya and Ellie had agreed on the perfect dress. It was Grecian style with a knotted waist, just below the bust line, which would allow the material to flow over Ellie's bump, no matter how big the baby was by then.

'Now the good bit, chocolate tasting time!' Freya linked her arm through Karen's as Ellie and Georgia followed on behind. She and Ollie wanted chocolate truffles as favours and there was an award-winning chocolatier at the wedding fayre offering tasting sessions, which was apparently a key duty of the bridesmaids, as well as for Karen, as stand-in mother of the bride. As always, Georgia would have to be careful about what she ate, but it was lovely to be included in everything, even if it meant she'd be fit for nothing the next day. That was how life with her condition was, and it was much easier coping with pacing herself at Seabreeze Farm, where just sitting and watching the comings and goings had become such a joy. It was going to be hard to leave when the time came, especially as Cliffview had fast become Ruby's home too.

'I'll catch up to you.' Ellie gestured over towards another stand. 'I just need to go and have a word with Norton's wine merchants to see if I can negotiate a deal to stock their new Kentish wine at the farm.'

'Okay, I'll let Freya know.' Georgia watched Ellie disappear into the crowd, before following the others, trying not to envy the look of excitement on the faces of the people moving from stall to stall, as they picked out the elements that would make up their perfect wedding. Georgia was really grateful to have the chance to be part of Freya and Ollie's big day and she was determined to make the most of it.

Caroline's eyes flew open as the ring tone on her phone burst into song. At some point, Georgia had changed it from a normal ringing sound to 'Summer Nights' by Olivia Newton-John and John Travolta, and Caroline had absolutely no idea how to change it back. Grabbing the phone off the bedside table, she glanced at the opposite side of the bed where Richard was stretched out, still fast asleep. Just as Georgia wanted, things were progressing much more quickly than Caroline had expected and, despite how much any child hated the thought of their middle-aged parent having a sex life, she knew her daughter would have approved. A phone call this early in the morning always sent a shiver down her spine, though, and she'd give up every moment of happiness she'd known, since meeting Richard, not to have constant worry about Georgia at the back of her mind every second of the day.

'Hello.' She was already breathless, as anxiety tightened around her chest.

'Don't worry, Caroline, it's only me.' Karen's voice had become familiar enough in the time since Georgia had been living at Cliffview for her not to have to introduce herself. She'd understood how important it was for Caroline to get a call every day, to let her know that her daughter was okay, without even having to be asked. Given how reluctant Georgia was to provide mundane updates herself, it had been especially welcome to hear from Karen on a regular basis. But she'd never called as early as this before.

'Can you hold on a sec? I'm just going to take this in the other room,' Caroline half-whispered, as she slipped out from under the covers, suddenly aware of how much crinkly skin her thigh-skimming negligee revealed in the cold light of day. Not that Richard seemed to notice, although he clearly needed a trip to the opticians, because according to him she was the most beautiful woman on earth. Thankfully he didn't even stir as she crept out of the bedroom, on to the landing and into Georgia's room, perching on the edge of the bed. She still thought of it as Georgia's room, even though she was living at Cliffview. As long as Caroline still lived in the house, it would always be Georgia's room no matter what. 'Sorry, Richard was still asleep and I didn't want to wake him.'

'Ooh, good for you!' Caroline could picture the expression on Karen's face as she spoke. 'I didn't wake you, did I?'

'No, I've been awake for ages.' It was a lie to spare Karen's embarrassment, but all Caroline wanted to know was why she was calling. Karen telling her not to worry was one thing, but she couldn't stop herself doing it until she knew for sure that Georgia was okay.

'Thank goodness, I've been holding off calling since I got the message at six, but I couldn't hold out any more.' Karen's words were coming out in a rush. 'Someone's come forward from the campaign who's willing to be a live kidney donor for Georgia.'

'You're joking.' Even as she said it, Caroline knew no-one could be that cruel, least of all Karen.

'No, it's true. Her name's Cindy and she's based in Canada. She's already had some blood tests over there, after approaching her doctors to see if she might be a match for Georgia, and the results are really positive. Apparently her doctors have been in touch with Georgia's consultant to discuss her initial results and they're going to run some more tests. Cindy said they'll get in touch with Georgia if the results are promising, but she contacted the campaign email address and said she wanted you to know there was hope in the meantime. I know the consultant said they wouldn't do a kidney transplant without the pancreas, but maybe Cindy's offer will change their minds?'

'God, I hope so! And it's not as if Georgia will be stopping someone else getting the kidney, if the woman only wants to donate to her. Does Cindy definitely want to do it? I'm not sure before all of this happened that I'd have been prepared to donate a kidney to a total stranger; in fact, I'm almost certain I wouldn't.'

'That's the thing, Cindy's been through something very similar to you. Her daughter has cystic fibrosis and a lung transplant from a deceased donor saved her life three years ago. She's been searching for a way to give something back since then and someone she knew shared one of my Facebook posts about Georgia.'

'I can't believe we've finally got some good news!' Caroline was still struggling to take it in. They were only half-way home, even if Cindy did turn out to be a match and the hospital agreed to the kidney transplant. But it felt like a massive step in the right direction and it would buy them more time. 'So has she got any idea about what might happen next?'

'I'll email you Cindy's details and you can talk to Georgia's consultant about how he wants to manage it around the tests they've got planned. But she wants to come over and meet Georgia as soon as possible.'

'Georgia's not going to like this. She only agreed to be the face of the campaign because she thought we might get some matches for other people; I don't think she ever really saw this as being a solution for her.' Caroline held the phone in one hand and grabbed a handful of Georgia's duvet in the other. She couldn't let her daughter throw away this opportunity, but no-one knew better than she did how pig-headed Georgia could be and she'd hate the thought of a stranger making this kind of sacrifice.

'I think that's why Cindy wants to come over and tell Georgia about her daughter, to try and help convince her how much it would mean to Cindy to be able to do it.' Karen had a determined tone. 'I know all of this is hard for Georgia, but so many people have shared the appeal and they all want to help her.'

'I know and thank you so much, we'd never have got this far

without you. It's something I can't ever repay.' The words were nowhere near enough. Caroline just wished she could stop shaking. She desperately wanted to share Karen's faith that they'd manage to persuade Georgia to accept this amazing gift. But knowing her daughter the way she did, that might still prove to be the biggest hurdle.

* * *

'Have you been crying?' The look on Gabe's face spoke volumes. They'd known each other for almost thirty years and even he could probably count on one hand the number of times he'd seen her cry since they'd left primary school. Georgia had long since decided that giving in to tears was something that could quickly get out of hand and she almost never cried in front of people, even when she'd been told she needed to go on dialysis and that her life was going to be severely restricted as a result. After the initial shock, she'd sobbed into her pillow in the dead of night, so that no-one else could hear her.

'Of course not.' Her red-rimmed eyes would have given her away no matter how hard she denied it, but that didn't stop her trying.

'What's wrong?' Gabe moved next to her on the veranda, slipping an arm around her shoulders which had already begun to shake with emotion again, despite her concentrating all her energies on trying to hold it back.

'Someone has come forward who wants to donate their kidney.'

'But that's great.' She could hear the joy in Gabe's voice, without having to see his face.

'No it's not. What if the hospital actually agree and something happens to her during the operation, or to her other kidney later on? And what if my body wrecks the kidney she's donated? She'll have risked her life for nothing.' The guilt was already so overwhelming that Georgia couldn't even think about herself, or the little voice that had whispered in her ear, every time she'd thought about getting a transplant: *and what about if it kills you too?*

'It won't.'

'You can't know that!' Georgia's voice rose, making Ruby jump off the chair she'd been sitting on and start circling her legs, picking up on the tension. Her fur was already damp with Georgia's tears; the poor little thing was probably going to end up traumatised. 'The only thing that's stopping me freaking out completely is the fact that I'm sure the hospital won't go ahead unless they find a pancreas that's a match for me, but for some reason they can't use the kidneys from the deceased donor. The odds of that have to be tiny, don't they? Especially given how hard it is to find a match in the first place.'

'It's amazing that a stranger wants to do this for you for a start. And it gives you other options if they find a pancreas that's a match, but the donor's kidneys are too damaged to use because of how they died. Mr Kennedy said that happens sometimes, didn't he? The only thing that matters is that people want to help and they're signing up to the register. All we need to do now is wait for a second donor.'

'You want someone to die so I can live?' Georgia was shouting now, but she couldn't help it. Holding on to her emotions for so long had created the perfect storm, all because a stranger living half-way around the world was willing to put their own life on the line for her. But Georgia didn't deserve it; she was nothing special.

'If that's what it takes, then, yes, I want that to happen.

People die every day, George, and most of the time they die and nothing good comes out of it. But eventually that's going to happen to someone who'd be in a position to save you, and it might even give their family and friends a tiny bit of comfort.' He took a shaky breath. 'I don't want to lose you. I can't stand the thought of it. If that makes me the worst person in the world, then I'm the worst person in the world.'

'So am I, because I don't want to go either. I don't want to leave Mum, or Ruby, but most of all I don't want to leave you.' Something inside Georgia had broken loose when Caroline had rung to break the news about Cindy's offer. All the bravado she wore like a protective layer was a lie. She wanted to live and she wanted a 'normal' life, whatever that was, one without all the restrictions her illness had piled on. The wall she'd spent a lifetime building up seemed to have come crumbling down and her deepest, darkest secret – the one she'd been certain she'd take to the grave with her – was tumbling out too. 'When I kissed you, it wasn't accident. I'm sorry, I never meant for this to happen, but I love you.'

'Then do this, George. Say yes to this, if you get the chance. Do it for everyone who loves you, including me. Because I love you too, I always have.' Gabe tilted her head slightly, kissing away the tears that were still falling.

Whatever happened next, things were never going to be the same between them and that was almost more terrifying than allowing a total stranger to make a life-changing sacrifice. But knowing that he loved her too meant there was more to lose than ever.

11

Georgia had never felt so sick, even straight after finishing a dialysis session. There was no anti-nausea medication that could be prescribed for meeting the person who was willing to give up one of their kidneys to save her life. What if she met Georgia and decided not to bother? Or Cindy turned out to be really awful, the sort of person who'd make a random racist comment without even thinking about it? Not that someone altruistic enough to give up their kidney for a stranger was likely to have that sort of personality defect. But if she did, Georgia wasn't sure she wanted any of that DNA becoming part of her. The thoughts swirling through her head were as uncontrollable as they were crazy and she just wanted to get the meeting over with.

Travelling up to London to see her consultant took less than two hours, door to door, but this time the journey felt interminable. Her mother and Gabe were with her, as they always were when she went up to see Mr Kennedy, but she couldn't join in with their conversation. She couldn't care less that one of their old neighbours had won a share of the lottery jackpot with the rest of the shop floor staff at the factory where they worked, or the fact that Kelsea Bay had been given a blue flag award for the cleanliness of its beach for the tenth year running. Meeting Cindy was all she could think about.

She stared out of the taxi window on the journey between the station and the hospital and they passed enough landmarks to give any tourist plenty of material to fill their Instagram feed. But she didn't really see any of them. She only ever came to London to see her consultant, since she got her dialysis at the local hospital in Elverham, and it was usually a bit of a treat to be in the city for a little while and have a change of scene. But not today.

'We're here.' Caroline had already handed the taxi driver the money for the fare and opened the door.

'Are you okay?' Gabe turned to Georgia when she didn't follow her mother.

'I don't know if I'm ready for this. I don't want to let everyone down. What if she doesn't like me and she changes her mind after she's met me?'

'Of course she's going to like you.' Gabe took hold of her hand and she looked up at him.

'We can't. We agreed not to tell anyone about us.' Georgia wanted to hold his hand more than she ever had, but the pressure of anyone knowing about them would be too much on top of everything else.

'Does it really matter if people know, with all the other stuff that's going on?' Gabe fixed her with a look. He was probably the most easy-going person she'd ever met and she couldn't remember him ever arguing with her when she'd been dead set on something. He was right, though, it didn't matter, and holding his hand made her feel a hundred times better the instant she did it.

'Okay then, I think I'm ready.' As Georgia answered, the taxi driver cleared his throat, no doubt wanting the couple still hanging around in the back of his cab to get a move on, so he could get to his next job. 'Let's do it.'

If Caroline noticed the fact that her daughter was holding her best friend's hand, then she didn't say anything. Her mum was almost certainly as nervous as Georgia and just desperately trying to hide it with cheerful conversation about whatever came into her head. Even in the lift up to Mr Kennedy's office on the third floor, where they'd also be meeting Cindy, she was talking about whether or not to splash out on a pair of wedge sandals she'd seen online. Gabe, to his credit, was doing a good job of not just answering, but sounding as if he was genuinely interested in whatever decision Caroline might ultimately reach.

'Oh God, I think that's her.' Georgia could see the row of chairs outside Mr Kennedy's office as soon as they stepped out of the lift. There was only one person sitting on the row, a woman with a neat blonde bob, just like the one in Cindy's photos on the social media profile Karen had shared with them. Up until that moment, a part of Georgia had wondered if this would all turn out to be an elaborate hoax. But, if that wasn't Cindy, then by some huge coincidence her absolute doppelganger was sitting outside Mr Kennedy's office.

'Hi.' It was a bald little word, but there was no handbook telling Georgia what to say to someone trying to save her life.

'Georgia, oh my God! Is it really you? You look even prettier than in the photos your mom sent me!' Cindy was immediately on her feet, wrapping her arms around Georgia, as if they were long lost family instead of total strangers.

'We can never thank you enough for this.' Caroline grabbed hold of Cindy as soon as she had the chance. 'You're amazing.'

'It's so nice to finally meet you.' Poor Cindy sounded as if she could barely catch her breath, given how tightly Caroline was holding on to her, but somehow she was still managing to talk. 'I'm just really grateful I've got the chance to help and give something back, after the gift we were given that saved Avril's life.'

'How's she doing since the operation?' Until now, Georgia had never given life after getting a transplant a lot of thought. There had always been so little possibility of it ever actually happening that she'd never been able to picture herself on the other side of the operation having survived.

'She's doing awesome.' Cindy's smile said it all. 'She's been offered a place at Oxford University, which has been her dream for as long as I can remember. Of course I'm terrified, and I could only deal with her coming at all by getting a rental place in Oxford for her first year. I run my own online business, designing bespoke jewellery, so I'm lucky I can work anywhere in the world. My husband, Brad, and Avril's sister, Celine, will come over for a vacation, whenever Celine has a break from school, but I couldn't relax if Avril was here on her own.'

'Does she still need a lot of care?' It was almost impossible for Georgia to imagine a life without constant intervention from medical professionals. She'd made friends with a few children who'd had cystic fibrosis, when she'd been in and out of hospital as a child, so she'd seen first-hand how much was involved in managing Avril's condition.

'It's not a cure, but it's given her a far healthier pair of lungs and she can live a much more normal life as a result. She was always this ball of energy, trapped inside a body that couldn't keep up, but now she's got the chance to live out some of her dreams, including coming to live in the UK, where my parents were originally from. She could barely have got any farther away from me and I think that was the idea! Once I've seen that she's coping okay and getting the support she needs in her first year of college, we've agreed that I'll go back home and I don't think she can wait for that.' Cindy rolled her eyes. 'What about you? What are you going to do if you get your transplant?'

'I honestly don't know.' Georgia felt like an idiot, standing in front of the woman who was giving up so much, with absolutely no idea of what she'd do as a result of the gift. 'I just want to have choices I guess. In a weird sort of way, despite being told that this will almost certainly be my last summer if I don't get a double transplant, the last few months have been the best of my life. I'm living in a place I could never have dreamed of. I'm painting and drawing all the time, and Gabe and I have even got a publishing deal for the children's stories we've been writing. Then there's Ruby of course.'

'Ruby?'

'She's the rescue dog that Gabe bought me for my birthday.' Cindy waited as Georgia scrolled through her phone. Not that it was hard to find a picture of Ruby, almost every photo she'd taken on her phone since Ruby had arrived, featured her in one way or another. She'd only had three things on her not-a-bucket list when she'd told Gabe about it, and they'd all been achieved. She just hoped that didn't mean she was done, because she was nowhere near ready to go yet.

The meeting with Mr Kennedy had gone well, as far as Georgia could tell. He'd said the results from the tests run by Cindy's hospital suggested she was the closest thing to a perfect match they were ever likely to find outside of Georgia's immediate family. The fact that she would be living in the UK for the next year gave them a good window of opportunity to find a donor for the pancreas and still have the option of using Cindy's kidney if they needed to. Mr Kennedy had explained that if Cindy had still been living in Canada, it would have made the double transplant almost impossible. The severity of Georgia's diabetes meant the new kidney almost certainly wouldn't last without an accompanying transplant and, with her heart in its weakened state, Mr Kennedy didn't think they could risk two separate transplants close together. He'd also admitted there was no chance of the kidney transplant being approved on its own, but then Georgia had never really expected that. They still needed to find a pancreas and, if they could use the kidney from that donor too, it would mean she'd never need the amazing gift Cindy had offered her. Whatever happened, she'd be eternally grateful for the sacrifice Cindy was willing to make.

When Mr Kennedy had told Cindy he wanted to run through the potential risks with her, should the kidney donation go ahead, she'd asked if the others could leave. When Georgia had protested and said she didn't want Cindy to go through with it, without knowing what she'd be risking, she'd agreed to let Caroline stay, but only her.

'There'll be a tiny risk to me, but I already know that.' Cindy had given Georgia an apologetic look. 'And that's a risk I'm more than willing to take. But from what I hear about you, even a tiny risk will put you off the idea?'

'You don't owe me anything, so how can I ask you to take a risk for me?'

'Listen honey, I've taken crazy risks for no good reason over the years. Everything from riding on the back of my boyfriend's Harley when I was in college, without a helmet, to bungee jumping on a holiday to Sydney when I turned forty! Every operation has risks and I've had a fair few over the years that I didn't need to have, including helping these defy gravity.' Cindy pointed to her chest and grinned. 'So taking a similar risk to do something amazing seems like nothing to me. If Mr Kennedy comes up with something I've never heard before, then you've got to trust me and your mom to weigh that up with a much more balanced view than you.'

'Mum's not known for her objectivity when it comes to me.' Georgia sighed. 'But she does always keep her promises. So if she promises me she won't let you take more than a tiny risk, then I'll leave the two of you to discuss it with Mr Kennedy.'

'I promise.' Caroline was already shoving Georgia out of the room, before she had a chance to change her mind. She'd seen the disappointment on her mother's face when Mr Kennedy had reiterated that there'd be no kidney transplant unless they got a match for the pancreas too. Her mother had been holding on to a hope she'd known was slim at best, so Georgia couldn't take this away from her too. They were one step closer to the possibility of a transplant, but there were still no guarantees. If a tiny part of her was glad there was less risk of her being taken away from Gabe as a result, she couldn't feel guilty. She'd waited half her life to tell him she loved him and, if all she was going to get was the rest of the summer to prove that to him, she didn't want it to be cut short.

To kill the time while they waited, they'd gone for a cup of tea in the café. When they'd come back and knocked on the door of Mr Kennedy's office, twenty minutes later, there'd been no response. Gabe had spotted Cindy along the corridor, talking animatedly into her mobile, but there'd been no sign of Caroline or Mr Kennedy.

'Maybe we should go back down to the reception desk and see if Mum's waiting there? I'm getting a bit worried about her.'

Georgia was starting to panic that it had all got too much for her mum: the build-up of emotion and the disappointment that there still might not be a transplant. Caroline had been to hell and back, as a wife and a mother, and had stayed strong throughout, but everyone had their breaking point.

'I expect she's already booked a cab to go out to lunch somewhere.' He'd barely got the words out of his mouth before Georgia heard the sound of a woman crying. She'd heard the sound often enough over the years – far too often – to have any doubt about who the tears belonged to, even if she hadn't caught a glimpse of the back view of her mother, through the slightly ajar door of a consulting room, half-way down the corridor from Mr Kennedy's office.

'I really thought this was going to be it, that we'd finally found the answer we've been longing for.' Caroline was half talking, half sobbing, and taking shuddering breaths in between, as Georgia stopped about six feet from the door.

'But the donor's a good match, isn't she?' A nurse in a dark blue uniform had her arm around Caroline, neither of them noticing the young couple outside in the corridor.

'Uh huh. But Mr Kennedy still thinks there's almost no chance of finding a donor for the pancreas before Georgia's heart is too weak to get through the operation. Even though Cindy coming forward means he doesn't need to wait for a donor whose kidneys are transplantable too. If he's right, then my baby's only got a few months left. I can't watch that happen! I want it to be me.'

'Oh Caroline, I'm so sorry. But don't forget what he said – this gives Georgia a better chance than she'd have had otherwise. You've got to try and hold on to that.'

'I know, but how can I look her in the face and try to sound as optimistic as I did this morning, when all I want to do is cry?'

'We should go.' Georgia whispered the words, turning back towards the lift before Gabe even had a chance to answer. She couldn't face seeing her mum and trying to hold it all together for her sake, not before she'd got her head around it. And she had no idea where to start.

* * *

The journey back from London was even more strained than the journey up there. Caroline had a rictus grin that must have been hurting her face long before they got out of the cab from the hospital back to the station. When her mother had suggested they make the most of the day out and go for lunch, with a false brightness that Georgia would have seen through even if she hadn't known the reason behind it, she'd feigned tiredness. It had given her an excuse to close her eyes and lean against the window, pretending not to hear the whispered conversation between her mum and Gabe.

Caroline hadn't confided in Gabe about what Mr Kennedy had told her, and Gabe would never betray Georgia and tell her mother that they already knew how low the chances still were of her getting a transplant. If a sliver of hope was all they had, then the least she could do was help her mum hold on to that, by never talking about the alternative. As hard as it had been to hear how long her odds still were, Georgia was glad she knew and she was more determined than ever to make the most of every single second.

'How are you doing?' Gabe put a cup of tea on the table in front of Georgia, five minutes after they finally got home to Cliffview. Rain was lashing against the windows and she could hear the roar of the waves crashing against the cliffs below them, even over the sound of Ruby snoring on her lap. For once there was no chance of sitting out on the veranda and making the most of the view.

'I'm fine.' She didn't miss the look of disbelief that crossed his face, but she meant what she'd said. 'I really am okay. This almost feels more normal, knowing where the end point is, where it's been since I saw Mr Kennedy in January. The whole idea of getting a transplant from Cindy knocked me for six and I was struggling with it. I've got to admit I let myself get a tiny bit excited at the thought of no more dialysis and having more time with the people I love, but I came to terms with this a long time ago and I'd rather know the reality than live in false hope. At least this way I can keep grabbing every moment I've got left, like I've been doing all summer, instead of wasting time holding out for something that's not going to happen.'

'There's still a chance...'

'Gabe, don't, *please*. I've always been able to rely on you. Don't let me down when I need you most.'

'Okay.' He shook his head, but there was still a glimmer of something in his eyes. He wanted to believe there was a chance and, if that helped him, Georgia wasn't going to be the one to take that away from him, any more than she would her mum.

'Let's not talk about it. I think it's easier on all of us that way.'

'Whatever you want, but you know I'm here for you if you need me.'

'I know.' Georgia edged along the sofa, moving closer towards him, until Ruby slid off her lap and wedged between them, still snoring contentedly. In this little world they'd created, it was easy to pretend that the summer was never going to end.

'I think that dog could sleep through anything, given that she manages to sleep through the sound of her own snoring.'

Gabe had got almost as good as Georgia over the years at glossing over reality and he laughed as Ruby let out an ear-splitting snort, making it sound as if the distant thunder that had been rumbling for the last hour was suddenly overhead.

'She's beautiful and I won't have anyone say otherwise.'

'I still think you should have called her Cyclops.' Gabe laughed again as Georgia shot him a look of disgust. He might pretend that he didn't adore Ruby every bit as much as her, but she'd caught him singing to the little dog in the mornings, and cutting up strips of chicken into tiny slivers that even Ruby, with her incredible overbite, didn't find too much of challenge. He'd take really good care of her when Georgia was gone and she was glad that Gabe would have Ruby too. Not that Georgia was under the illusion that losing her was something he'd never get over, but it would be hard for a while. She wouldn't be the love of his life, the way he was hers, but then she never would have been, even if she'd lived to be eighty.

If Georgia hadn't beaten him to it by dying, Gabe would eventually have found someone else who shared his spirit of adventure more than Georgia did. His dream job was working for National Geographic, travelling to far flung places, off the beaten track, capturing the sort of once-in-a-lifetime photographs that he'd never get by staying in Kent. As much as she'd dreamt of having amazing holidays across the world and catalogued them on the list she'd made with Gabe, back when they'd been in sixth form, that was all her idea of travelling had been. Even if Georgia had been given the choice of settling permanently anywhere in the world, she'd still have chosen Kelsea Bay and that would never truly be enough for Gabe. Maybe it was another blessing to come out of all the bad stuff, the fact that they'd never be faced with their dreams pulling them in totally different directions, and having to make an impossible choice. When she was gone, Gabe could live his dreams without a shred of guilt.

'If you insult my dog again, you can go back to sleeping in the spare room.' Colour rose up Georgia's neck as she spoke. She'd never been skilled at flirting and banishing Gabe to the spare room as a punishment, even in jest, felt like she was making some kind of sexual innuendo. Their relationship had moved into unchartered territory after they'd both said the L word, and Gabe had been careful to make sure it was all on Georgia's terms. She always had to make the first move and, when they'd finally slept together, it had been incredible, at least from her perspective. The best bit had been falling asleep and waking up in Gabe's arms, though. Maybe prizing that above sexual intimacy should have been a stage they didn't reach for years, but it was already Georgia's happy place.

'If you're going to make me sleep in the spare room, there's something I need to ask you first.' Gabe moved and Ruby let out a grunt as she unceremoniously tipped upside down like a woodlouse on its back, sliding into the space Gabe had left on the sofa before scrabbling to right herself.

'What are you doing?'

'This.' Gabe had dropped to one knee in front of her, and Georgia's first reaction was to burst out laughing. He was just messing about, he had to be. 'That's not the sort of reaction I was hoping for when I decided to ask you to marry me.'

'Gabe—' She was still laughing but his face was perfectly straight, and suddenly her cheeks were flushed with heat again. She didn't know what to think, but there was a chance he was actually serious.

'Georgia Meredith Banks. I've loved you since we were at infants' school, when we used to have pretend weddings in the playground at least three times a week.' Gabe was smiling now.

'It's time to make good on a promise that's nearly twenty-five years overdue and marry me for real.'

'I seem to remember there was always an old curtain ring involved in your proposals back then.' She had to keep teasing him, because she still didn't want him to see her cry, even if they were happy tears.

'You read my mind.' Gabe pulled an old brass curtain ring out of his pocket, which looked exactly how she remembered. 'Now I've come up with the goods, is that a yes?'

'Why not?' Georgia laughed again as he slipped the ring onto her finger, a much snugger fit than it had been all those years ago, and folded her in to his arms. She let herself pretend just for a moment that this really was the start of forever. It was another reason to be glad she'd overheard her mum's conversation with the nurse. If she thought she'd have a chance of living a long life, or even one that might last beyond another year or two, she'd never have been able to say yes, no matter how much she wanted to. She couldn't have deprived Gabe of finding the love of his life and fulfilling all the dreams she could never be a part of. But this way, she got to marry the love of her life and it was barely more of a commitment to him than those proposals back in the infants' school playground. It would be over before he knew it and he'd be free to move on, the way he always would have done eventually. Except now she wouldn't be left with a broken heart.

12

The date would probably have been significant to Georgia, even if it hadn't been her wedding day. There was only one month to go until her stay at Cliffview was over and it was exactly one month since Gabe had proposed. They'd given notice for the wedding at the registry office the day after he'd slipped the curtain ring onto her finger. One Wish had immediately offered to step in and organise the wedding, as soon as they'd heard about the proposal, but it wasn't what Georgia wanted. The charity needed to use its resources elsewhere and she didn't want a big wedding anyway. What was important to her was for the people who meant the most to her in the world to be there.

When she'd asked Ellie if she could get married at the farm, her friend hadn't hesitated. They were getting married on a Wednesday, which had no chance of clashing with someone else's big day, in the gazebo that looked over the sea in one direction and Gerald and Dolly's field in the other. They'd be having a low key wedding breakfast in Gerry's tearooms, and Karen had insisted on closing it and the rest of the farm to the public for the day. After that, they'd have a few drinks back at Cliffview and, with less than thirty guests, including Ellie, Karen, Freya and their families, there was no need for lots of staff. Everyone at the wedding would be incredibly important to Gabe and Georgia, and the bottom line was that she would be marrying him, something that she'd never believed would be possible and it didn't need any bells and whistles.

The biggest surprise for Georgia had come three days after telling everyone that Gabe had proposed. When Ellie had turned up at Cliffview and called up to Georgia from the bottom of the access ramp, she had been sitting in her favourite spot on the veranda with Ruby curled up in her lap. It was the go-to position for both of them these days.

'Have you got a minute?' Ellie's baby bump had really started to blossom and it made the perfect resting place for the package she was holding in her arms.

'Of course, come up. Do you want a drink?'

'No, I'm fine, I've got to get back to put Mae to bed. Ben's on bath time duty tonight, but she's going through a phase where she'll only settle down with me.' Ellie gave an apologetic shrug. 'I just wanted to bring this over to you. I picked it up at the wedding fayre from ex-display stock that one of the dress retailers was selling off after the fashion show. I bought a few for when we next need to do an advertising shoot at the farm and I remembered you saying you liked this one.'

'Oh my God, when did you sneak off and do that?' Georgia lifted the lid off the box that Ellie had put on the table, instantly knowing which dress it was – the simple Bardot-style dress she'd fallen in love with.

'It was after I spoke to the wine merchant. Her sister runs one of the wedding boutiques exhibiting at the fayre and she asked me if I was interested in buying any of the ex-display dresses the models had been wearing. Like you, I thought this was the nicest dress there, so I couldn't resist. But don't feel you've got to wear it, if you've got something else in mind.'

'I hadn't even started to think about that, but I'd never find a dress I loved more. Thank you so much.' Ruby jumped off her lap as she got up to hug Ellie. 'Are you sure you don't mind me borrowing it? I don't want to ruin it before the photo shoot.'

'You can't borrow it, but you can have it. And if you even offer to pay me for it, I'll have to sling it over the edge of the cliff. It's yours, I think it always was. Call it serendipity or random coincidence, but you were obviously meant to have it and the girl who owns the boutique said she's happy to make any adjustments it needs.'

'It's perfect and you've all been so great since I moved here, I can never thank you enough for any of it.' Georgia wasn't going to argue with Ellie about accepting the dress. She just hoped that the book she and Gabe had written would raise enough money to pay everyone back for what they'd given her. The royalties from the book itself were going to One Wish, but they'd negotiated for the profits from any related merchandise that might be sold, including prints of her illustrations, to go towards the upkeep of the rescued animals at Seabreeze Farm, and the ongoing work that Ben's veterinary practice was doing with the rescue centre that had re-homed Ruby. The farm had just taken in twenty ex-battery hens and, if Georgia had learned anything about her new friends since moving to Cliffview, their latest rescue mission definitely wouldn't be their last.

As it had turned out, the dress hadn't needed much alter-ation, other than being taken in by a few inches. The seam-stress had made the excess material into a little collar for Ruby, who would be acting as bridesmaid. She was used to going almost everywhere with Georgia, except when she went to the hospital for dialysis, so there was no way she'd put up with being left in the house all day whilst the wedding went on without her.

To keep to tradition, Gabe had spent the night before the wedding back at home with his parents, having let out his flat after moving in with Georgia. Caroline had stayed at Cliffview with her daughter, and she would be the one walking Georgia down the aisle. Her mother had sewn a bit of blue material from one of Georgia's father's old shirts, inside the hem of her wedding dress, which meant her dad would get to be part of her big day too.

'Oh, love, you look beautiful.' Caroline's waterproof mascara was going to have its work cut out for it, if her first reaction was anything to go by.

'You look beautiful too, Mum.' Georgia let herself be folded into her mother's arms, breathing in the familiar scent of White Linen perfume, which was probably her favourite smell in the world because it reminded her of her mum even when they were apart.

'Are you ready, darling?' Caroline looked at her as she finally pulled away, and all Georgia could do was nod. She'd been ready to marry Gabe all those years ago, back in the infants' school playground, but she was more ready than ever now and she didn't want to waste another minute.

* * *

Caroline couldn't remember smiling as much as she had on the day of the wedding in years. For a long time there'd been so little to smile about, but this last summer at Seabreeze Farm seemed to have been bathed in eternal sunshine, literally and metaphorically. There might have been the occasional rainy day, but before Georgia had moved into Cliffview, life had started to feel like a non-stop rainy Monday. Especially since Mr Kennedy's prediction that there wouldn't be another summer for Georgia after this one. Caroline had expected the prognosis to make it impossible to enjoy the time they had left, but because of One Wish, everyone at the farm, and mostly because of Gabe, it had turned out to be the complete opposite of that.

Caroline had also cried more openly than she ever had in a single day, but for once the tears were mostly tears of joy and she didn't feel as if she had to hold them in for Georgia's sake. Her daughter was world champion of reining in her own emotions, but even she'd given in to tears a couple of times, once during the ceremony and once when Karen had brought out the wedding cake, which was a perfect sponge and fondant replica of Ruby.

'Does all this make you want to take the plunge again?' Karen came over to where Caroline had been standing on her own, watching Georgia and her new husband out on the balcony laughing with friends, their heads pressed together in a gesture of intimacy that couldn't be faked. Their engagement might have come out of the blue, but she'd known they loved each other and always hoped they might eventually admit it to themselves.

'I wouldn't completely rule out getting married again.' Caroline smiled as Karen topped up her glass with the champagne that just seemed to keep coming. She'd tried at least ten times to talk to Karen and Ellie about paying for the wedding, but they kept insisting that it was all taken care of through donations. The social and mainstream media coverage of the wedding, and the story behind it, which would only be released after it was all over, had apparently been enough for all of Seabreeze Farm's normal suppliers to donate goods and services for free. It would also help promote the ebook version of *Gerry and the Great Goat Escape*, Gabe and Georgia's children's story. The digital version had been fast tracked through the system by the publishers, to ride on the crest of the news about its authors getting married, made all the more newsworthy by Georgia's prognosis. As Georgia had so pragmatically put it: tragedy sells. Caroline shook the thought of those words off; she wasn't going to let Georgia's illness ruin what had been such a perfect day.

'I wouldn't let Georgia hear you say that. She'll be booking you and Richard in for a wedding on the next free date in the farm diary.'

'I don't think she's quite as pushy now that she's had a wedding of her own and she's going to be a bridesmaid for Freya in December. I'm surplus to requirements these days!'

'I doubt that.' Karen squeezed her arm. 'The two of you walking down the aisle together had me sobbing like a baby. Even Mae was better behaved than me!'

'She was brilliant and such a little cutie. I'm sure she'll be a fantastic big sister too, when the time comes. It must be so wonderful to look forward to having two grandchildren by the time Christmas comes around.' Caroline fought to keep the wistful tone out of her voice, but she hadn't quite managed it.

'I'm so lucky and I realise that now more than ever.' Karen squeezed her arm again. 'I just wish there was more I could do for Georgia. We all do.'

'You've done so much already, not least finding Cindy. All we can do now is wait and keep praying. I don't even know if I believe there's anything up there.' Caroline gestured skyward.

'But I'd pray to Jesus, Allah, Buddha, Shiva and the man in the moon if I thought there was any chance of it making a difference. We just have to make the most of each day, and that's been so much easier to do since Georgia moved to Cliffview.'

'You know when the original lease is up that we all want her to stay, as long as she wants to? It was meant to be a temporary arrangement that everyone could benefit from, but we didn't know back then that we were going to come to care about you all so much, and that you'd end up feeling like family.'

'The feeling's mutual.' Caroline's eyes filled with tears again. 'But she won't stay on beyond what was agreed, unless she pays the going rate. It's taken all Ellie's efforts to persuade her that we didn't need to pay for the wedding.'

'Georgia's so strong and I don't think I've ever met someone as determined as her. If anyone can get through the wait for a transplant and come out the other side, it's her.'

'I just hope she gets the chance.' Caroline hadn't told anyone what Mr Kennedy had said about the likelihood of that happening. Karen would probably have been the one person she'd have opened up to, if she hadn't worked so hard on the campaign to find Georgia a kidney donor. But if the music hadn't started up at that precise moment, she'd probably have weakened anyway and told her new friend just how scared she was that Georgia's time was going to run out before they found a donor for her pancreas transplant.

As it was, the strains to 'The Shoop Shoop Song' suddenly filled the room and she had to smile. It was the song that had been number one when Georgia and Gabe were both born, and she'd first met Gabe's mum at the post-natal classes being run at their local cottage hospital. It might not be a classic, but if they'd been born a few weeks later they'd have been stuck with 'I Wanna Sex You Up' and a few weeks earlier their song would have been

'Stonk' by Hale and Pace, a couple of middle-aged comedians who'd long since faded into obscurity. So, as corny as it was, the two of them had been lucky to end up with the cheesy anthem as their song, and it seemed fitting to have it for their first dance. Gabe had obviously organised it, with Alan and Richard grinning like school boys as they took on the role of DJs, making sure the song blasted out from the speaker someone had set up on the veranda.

Georgia was usually reluctant to do anything that made her the centre of attention, but she seemed prepared to make an exception for her wedding day. When Gabe held out his hand and asked her to dance, she didn't hesitate. Everyone was clapping along with the song and those who were old enough to remember it, including Caroline and Karen, were soon singing along too. When Cher reached the crescendo of the chorus, Gabe planted a kiss on Georgia's lips and everyone cheered. Caroline didn't know if anyone was filming it, but she was desperate to imprint the moment on her memory forever. The realisation that it might one day be all she had left, made her eyes fill with tears all over again.

Georgia flopped on to the bed, still wearing the wedding dress she'd never take off again if it was up to her. Ruby had already left her mark on it, in the form of paw prints and a silvery trail of slobber along the bottom hem, but it was still perfect to her.

'You look exhausted.' Gabe slipped off her shoes as he spoke.

'I am, but it's been fabulous, hasn't it? Even the dance to that bloody awful song!' She laughed at the memory of the whole crowd shoop shooping along to the music, whilst Gabe had spun her around the veranda in front of them all. If someone had told her that it was going to happen, she'd have cringed at the thought, but she'd ended up loving every moment.

'It's been great and you've done brilliantly. You barely sat down all day.'

'I was determined not to give in today, but I've got a feeling I might pay for it tomorrow.'

'Well you're supposed to spend your honeymoon in bed.' Gabe grinned, lying on the bed next to her and pushing the hair away from her face. 'I love you Mrs Ritchie.'

'I love you too.'

'Do you want anything before you go to sleep?'

'Only you.' Flirting with Gabe still felt so weird and she'd never been the sort of person to come out with a line like that. She probably couldn't have talked dirty to save her life and this was about as edgy as it was going to get.

'We don't have to, you're tired and loads of people are too exhausted on their wedding nights to—'

'I *want* to and we're not like most couples. They have thousands of nights when they can make up for missing out on their wedding night. We don't know how many nights we've got, but there definitely won't be thousands. We're not going to be old and grey together, when you might need little blue pills to give you a helping hand! So I want to make the most of every day we get together, especially tonight.' Georgia propped herself up on to one elbow and grinned. 'Unless you don't want to, of course, or you secretly already need those little blue pills long before your time.'

'Seeing you in that dress today did more for me than any pill could ever do and I certainly don't need any help.'

'You're going to see me out of this dress in a minute, so brace yourself.'

'I can't wait.' Gabe pulled her closer; the exhaustion that had washed over her, when the last of the wedding guests had said goodbye, was completely forgotten. She might only get a few months as Gabe's wife but they had tonight and, for now, that was all that mattered.

13

Georgia could count the number of times she'd had alcohol since starting dialysis on the fingers of one hand. It was allowed, but the complexity of balancing it with her medication and the limits on her other fluid intake, along with the risk of a hypo, meant it just wasn't worth it. She'd had half a glass of champagne for the toasts on the day of the wedding, but she certainly hadn't expected to have another drink for a long time, if ever. There'd been moments when she'd considered being reckless and not following the rules any more, after what Mr Kennedy had said about the likelihood of the transplants going ahead. But that wouldn't have been fair on everyone who was trying to help her, and who were still holding on to the hope that a miracle might happen. She was following the rules that had been part of her life for as long as she could remember and Gabe knew them almost as well as she did. So when he arrived home at Cliffview, waving a bottle of champagne, she couldn't help wondering what he was playing at.

'We've done it, George. I can't believe it!' Gabe put the

champagne on the kitchen island, bending down to make a fuss of Ruby, who was even more excited than usual to see him.

'Done what?' Sometimes, after dialysis, she had what she imagined a hangover would feel like and just thinking straight was like wading through treacle. Gabe had been on a shoot all day, so her mother had stepped in to take her to the hospital and for once she and Gabe hadn't been in constant contact over text or social media. Hopefully he'd had some good news from the shoot, but if he was finally getting the recognition he deserved for his talents it would have nothing to do with Georgia. He'd had to make a living since finishing his photography degree and drifting into wedding photography and portraiture had been a double-edged sword for him. The money could be good, but the further he went down that route the harder it was for him to keep trying to break through into photo journalism. He'd had some freelance shots published over the years, but his big break, the one that might allow him to follow his dream full time, still hadn't come. If now was the time, she'd definitely make an exception for a glass of champagne.

'We're number one!' She had no idea what he was talking about and Gabe had clearly registered the nonplussed look that must have crossed her face. 'With the book! It's number one in the Amazon ebook charts.'

'It can't be.' Gabe had to have got this wrong. The book had only been out for just over a week.

'Honestly, *look*.' Gabe showed her his phone. There was their book, *Gerry and the Great Goat Escape*, with a best-seller flag and a ranking of number one.

'How the hell did that happen?' Georgia was still staring at the screen, and the picture she'd painted of Holly, Gerald and Dolly, when she'd first moved to the farm, was staring back at her from the ebook cover.

'I rang Cassie and she said Fiaba had a big campaign push, but even they hadn't anticipated this. She thinks it was down to all the other publicity – from the wedding, the fundraising and the donor awareness campaign. Even she was shocked that it's taken off this quickly; they're rushing through the physical books now to get them into the shops.'

'Can you punch me on the arm? Just so I know this isn't one of those bizarre dreams I get when I eat too much cheese, or when I watch one of those weird Netflix documentaries you like so much too close to bed time!'

'I'm not going to punch you, but I will kiss you.' Gabe pulled Georgia into his arms, leaving her in no doubt she was awake. No matter how many times she'd dreamt about being with Gabe before it had finally happened, her imagination had never lived up to the reality.

'So what are we going to do to celebrate? We ought to let Ellie and the others know,' Georgia said, as she finally pulled away from Gabe. It was still almost impossible to believe, but maybe telling other people would be one way of making it feel more real.

'We can tell the others later, but I thought maybe we could keep it to ourselves tonight and have a little celebratory dinner?'

'What are you cooking?'

'That would be a punishment, not a celebration.' Gabe laughed.

'Yeah and getting hospitalised with food poisoning would be a unique way to celebrate!' Georgia couldn't help laughing too. Gabe had more talent than it was fair for any single person to have, but the only thing he'd successfully managed to cook since they'd moved in were the moules marinière, which had only really needed to be heated up with a bit of white wine and olive oil. Everything else he'd tried had been nothing short of disastrous. It was a flaw that she was glad he possessed, even if it meant takeaways when it was his turn to cook dinner, otherwise he'd have been in real danger of being perfect.

'I'll order in. What do you fancy?'

'Curry?'

He nodded in response to her suggestion, already opening the Just Eat app to put in their order. There was no need for him to ask what she wanted, he'd known her too long and too well to doubt she'd have anything other than what she always had. If it was possible to be aware of anything on the other side, she was going to miss him so much. Tonight was a celebration though, and they'd be doing it in style.

The outdoor sofa positioned at the end of the veranda had been a wedding gift from Ellie and her family. Georgia had every intention of leaving it behind when she left, but there were still ten days to go before they moved out of Cliffview and she wanted to squeeze every last second out of it. As she sat next to Gabe on the sofa, he pulled the faux fur throw around them and Ruby burrowed underneath it.

'I think the Star of Bengal surpassed themselves tonight, although I might not be able to move off this sofa even if there's an emergency.' Gabe patted his stomach.

'Why would you ever want to move?' There was nowhere she'd rather have been in that moment. The sky and the sea before them were somewhere between indigo and black, with a blanket of stars offering a golden contrast to the darkness. Only that contrast, and the motion of the waves below, gave a clue to where the sky ended and the sea began. It felt as if they were looking out towards the entire universe.

'I don't want to move; I'd be happy to stay here forever.' Gabe put an arm around her shoulders and she knew what was coming next. 'Have you thought any more about Alan's offer?'

'We can't stay here, however much I'd love to. It's someone else's turn to experience the magic of Cliffview. Being here has already given me everything I ever dreamt of and some things I didn't even realise I wanted.' Georgia turned to him and smiled. 'I'd never have had the arrogance to even dream about illustrating a bestselling book.'

'It just shows there are things you think could never happen that actually can.' Gabe lowered his voice. 'I know you don't believe there's any chance of the transplant happening, but I really think it will.'

'Let's not talk about that again.' Sometimes the most exhausting part of Georgia's illness was keeping up the pretence that everything was going to be okay for everyone else's sake. Agreeing with Gabe that there was a chance of the transplant going ahead wasn't just exhausting, it could be dangerous too, if it meant they didn't have the conversation they really needed to have before it was too late. 'How did the photoshoot go today? You never said.'

'It was really good, but it got a bit side-lined by the news about the book.'

'But you finished the shoot first, didn't you?'

'Yes and they were really pleased with the initial review of the shots.' Gabe had been taking photographs at a conservation centre for a big wildlife charity campaign. It was the sort of job that could really help raise his profile and open the door to the type of work he wanted to do, but he was obviously playing it down.

'If you get offered other work off the back of this, I want you to promise me you'll take it, even if it's overseas. No matter what's going on with me.'

'I'm not going anywhere.' Gabe's tone was even, but there was a steely resolve in his voice all the same. If this was going to turn into a battle of wills, then she'd just have to win.

'Whatever you want to believe, I'm not going to be here forever and I can't stand the thought that you'll be paying the price long after I'm no longer around, because you're turning down opportunities when they come along.'

'Georgia—'

'This is important.' She cut him off, shrugging his arm off too. 'I want you to promise me, the same way you promised you'll always make sure Ruby is looked after, that you'll move on when the time comes and that you'll make the most of every chance you're given. It's up to you to do it for both of us.'

'I don't need to, because things are going to be okay. I can feel it.'

'Just promise me, if the worst happens, that you'll get on with your life. Otherwise this marriage is going to be shorter than the average spur-of-the-moment Vegas drive through.'

'Okay, I promise. Now can we talk about something else please?' All the light that had been in Gabe's eyes, when he'd told her about the book, had gone out and she hated being responsible for that. It was for his own good though and she was doing it because she loved him, despite how devastating it would be to let him go even a moment sooner than she had to. Summer was coming to an end far too quickly, but sooner or later he had to move on and she had to make sure he was ready, whatever it took from her. He'd never broken a promise to Georgia yet and she'd just have to trust him on this one too.

* * *

There were only two days to go until Georgia was due to move out of Cliffview and, despite Ellie's numerous attempts to beg her to stay on, she wouldn't even discuss it. Ellie couldn't imagine anyone but Georgia and Gabe living at the cabin and, when Karen had said that they felt like part of the family, it hadn't been an exaggeration. The book they'd written had spread the word about Seabreeze Farm all over the world, and they had bookings and enquiries stretching years ahead already. Even when Ellie had sat up late into the evening with Ben, coming up with a set of financial projections to prove to Georgia and Gabe that their promotion of the farm would more than cover the cost of renting Cliffview for the next year, Georgia had still just shrugged it off. Ellie could understand why she didn't want to feel like a charity case and she'd made that clear from the moment the suggestion of staying at Cliffview had been put to her, but she was the furthest thing from being a charity it was possible to be. Almost every day she'd been at Cliffview, Georgia had taken the opportunity to do something that made a positive difference, not just to life at the farm but to the work of One Wish. And today wasn't going to be any different.

'What time will he be here?' Georgia looked at Ellie as they stood outside Gerry's tearooms. It was another beautiful sunny day and, for once, England seemed to be enjoying an Indian summer despite having already experienced a fantastic run of good weather from April through to August.

'Any minute now.' Ellie looked at her watch, nerves fluttering in her stomach. Since starting to work with One Wish there'd been a few requests from children who wanted to visit the farm and spend time with the animals, and it always felt like a huge responsibility to make their day as perfect as it could possibly be. Today they'd be welcoming Joel, a little boy with muscular dystrophy who was obsessed with donkeys. He'd instantly become Georgia and Gabe's biggest fan, after his mother had downloaded their book on the first day it was released. When she'd tweeted a picture of Joel's delighted face, as he read the story, and tagged One Wish in the picture, it had been picked up by the team and a visit to the farm swiftly arranged. He'd be meeting Georgia and Gabe too, and the plan was for Georgia to sketch a picture of Joel with the animals, to give him a lasting memory of his big day.

'I'm really nervous; I hope he's not disappointed when he meets us!' Georgia's words echoed what Ellie had been thinking. 'Although we can rely on Gerald and the others to keep him entertained, even if we let the side down.'

'That's true. Oh here we go.' Ellie took a deep breath as the minivan swept into the car park. A few minutes later, Joel's wheelchair had been unloaded from the back of the vehicle and all the introductions had been made.

'What would you like to do first? We can go down to meet Gerald and the others? Or there's some cake and special treats for you in the tearoom?'

'The donkeys, please!' Joel, who they'd been told was seven years old, had the biggest smile that Ellie had ever seen and even though his condition had already severely affected his mobility, he was still managing to bounce up and down in his wheelchair.

'Come on then, let's go.' Ellie's nerves had disappeared, in the wake of Joel's infectious excitement. 'You can help me make some lunch for Gerald and the other donkeys and they'll be your friends for life. Georgia's going to draw a picture of you feeding them too, so you can take it home.'

'This is going to be the best day ever!' Joel had everyone smiling from the moment he arrived and Gabe took hundreds of photos, documenting every special moment. They spent a good few hours out on the farm and Joel was even able to brush Gerald's coat, still sitting in his wheelchair. Thankfully his hands seemed far less affected by his condition than his lower body. Gerald was happy to be groomed, as long as the bucket he had his head in was regularly re-filled with feed, which meant he was almost as happy as the little boy. When Joel eventually started to show signs of getting tired, they all went back to Gerry's tearoom for a little buffet. The pièce de résistance was a cake that Karen had made, which looked like a cartoon version of Gerald lying down in his field. Between that and the pug cake she'd made for Georgia and Gabe's wedding, Karen was getting to be dab hand at recreating the animals of Seabreeze Farm in sponge and fondant.

'I think he's enjoyed the day, don't you?' Ellie was sitting with Georgia and Gabe, watching as Joel tucked into a second piece of cake.

'If he's enjoyed it half as much as I've enjoyed sharing the day with him, then I'd say it was a success.' Georgia smiled, but before anyone had the chance to answer, her phone started to ring.

'What is it?' Ellie saw the smile slide off Georgia's face as soon as she looked down at her phone screen.

'It's the number of the transplant team that the hospital gave me.' Georgia looked at Ellie, before turning to Gabe. 'It can't be, though, can it?'

'Just answer it and we'll deal with whatever they say.' Gabe sounded much calmer than he must have felt, given how hard

Ellie's heart was hammering against her ribcage. This could be the call that changed everything for Georgia, or it could be nothing at all. Holding her breath as Georgia picked up the call, Ellie looked at Gabe. This meant everything to him and Ellie was praying harder than she ever had that it would be the news they'd all been waiting for.

14

Georgia's hands were shaking. She'd thought about writing letters to her mum and Gabe, but she probably couldn't have held a pen, let alone have formed a cohesive sentence on paper. She'd left a voicemail for Cindy, thanking her with all her heart for the gift she'd offered and letting her know that the hospital had matched her with a donor whose pancreas and kidney she'd be receiving.

The only good thing about being ill for so long was that there'd been plenty of opportunities to tell the people who were important to her how she felt about them. She'd told her mum many times how grateful she was that she'd had Caroline as a parent. She might have been incredibly unlucky health wise, but she'd won the lottery when it came to mothers. There was not much she'd left unsaid, even before it was all systems go for the transplant. The trouble was, she still hadn't been completely honest with Gabe. He knew she loved him, but he had no idea how much. She hadn't wanted to put that level of pressure on him, to make him feel like he had to return that depth of feeling, if he couldn't. A part of her was terrified that, even if the operation was a success, the life she'd always wanted with him could be taken away. As strange as it might seem, it suddenly felt easier to focus on what might go wrong than to face up to what the long-term consequences might be if everything went right. One thing she wanted to be certain of was that Gabe, being her next of kin, wouldn't make any more sacrifices for her than he already had.

'Gabe, I need you to promise me that if there's any chance of me being left with brain damage if something goes wrong, I won't be kept alive with a machine.'

'George—'

'We've got to talk about it, Gabe, *please*. It's no good saying that nothing like that's going to happen, because we both know it could.'

'I can't do it George, I can't promise you that I'll just let them switch the machines off and that I'll be ready to say my goodbyes to you, if it comes to that, because I'm never going to be ready.'

Gabe was openly crying and she reached out and took his hand. She needed him to understand this. The transplant had always been the holy grail, her one chance of having a normal life, and Gabe had been overjoyed at the news when they'd first got the call, punching the air as if he'd won the lottery. If the transplant failed it would be easy for her and she'd probably never know a thing about it. She wouldn't have to face the gradual fade out she'd feared more than anything, dying slowly in a bed where she knew she was saying her last goodbyes to the people who meant the most to her. The fears she'd had about having the operation seemed to have disappeared the moment she'd heard the words: *we've found a match*. She was so close to the point where time was running out anyway that, even if she died during the operation, what she'd be robbed of could probably be measured in weeks. There was less pressure than there might have been with a living donor, too, and of risking letting them down if the transplant wasn't a success. The family of the deceased donor would have their heartbreak compounded if the transplant didn't work, but they'd already faced the worst kind of heartbreak imaginable, so the stakes didn't feel quite as high. The only thing she was scared of now was letting Gabe and her mother down, by allowing them to sacrifice everything to keep her alive at any cost.

'You can and you've never let me down before, but I need to know before I can go into the op that you'll do what we've agreed. I've spent all my life being a patient and being restricted by my health. If I'm left really damaged by this, and I can't even think for myself, I don't want to be here any more. I've managed to make the most of the life I've got, especially this last summer, but I don't want to live at any cost.' She wouldn't let them take her down for the operation until he'd promised her that he'd do as she asked. If things went wrong, it would be over and, if they went right, there was a whole world of possibilities waiting for her. If there were things that terrified her about that, she wasn't even going to think about them until she'd heard his promise.

'I understand what you're saying.' He still couldn't look at her and she squeezed his hand, imprinting the memory of his touch. If this was the last time, she wanted to take it with her.

'And you promise not to keep me alive if I'm not going to have any quality of life?' Her eyes didn't leave his face and eventually he nodded.

'I promise. But it's not a decision I'm going to have to make.'

'We never really thought we'd get to the transplant stage, did we?' She caressed the back of his hand with her thumb. If the transplant succeeded, it would mean that she and Gabe might have something closer to the length of life together other people took for granted when they said their wedding vows. She wanted that more than anything, but it hadn't been the deal when she'd accepted Gabe's proposal and she had no idea how he felt about it. 'Would you have proposed if you'd known that we might have a lot longer than we thought?'

'Of course I would.' He furrowed his brow. 'Are you saying you wouldn't have said yes?'

'I never dreamt this might actually happen, not after Mr Kennedy's prediction.' Georgia couldn't answer the question, not without revealing more to him than she wanted to. She wouldn't admit what the chance of 'forever' meant to her, not when she couldn't really be sure how he felt. 'But I don't regret a moment we've spent together.'

'That's good, because you're stuck with me now.' Gabe smiled, but she couldn't help scanning his face, trying to work out if there was something else hidden there. She didn't want him to feel trapped if the transplant was successful. No-one wanted to be the bad guy who walked out on the girl who'd finally had the life-saving operation they never believed would happen.

'If something does go wrong, I want you to make me another promise.' She ignored his frown. This had to be done whether he liked it or not. 'I want you to make sure you take every opportunity that comes your way to further your career. I've spoken to Mum and she said she'll always look after Ruby if you need her to when you're away working, and Barney would probably love the company, even if she does get on his nerves a bit.'

'I'm not going anywhere without you.'

'But if I'm not here...'

'Okay, I promise, now can we *please* talk about something else?'

'What did you have in mind? I could tell you what happened in *Peaky Blinders*.' She grinned, knowing what his reaction would be even before he put his hands over his ears.

'Don't you dare!' They'd both been addicted to the series since they'd been late to the party and they'd gradually been working their way through, but Georgia was half a season ahead because of how busy he'd been with work over the summer.

'Or we could talk about your haircut.' Georgia pulled a face, defaulting to the humour they always used to avoid the emotions bubbling dangerously close to the surface. She might not be afraid of the operation any more, but suddenly being a whole new person on the other side of the transplant held its own fears. 'If you were going to go for something like that, you could at least have got sponsored for One Wish!'

'It's the last time I go to a new barbers. If they're still in business by this time next month then there's no justice in the world. I mean it's not as if I asked for anything difficult and now I look like I've had a lobotomy.' Gabe laughed, seemingly equally grateful to lighten the mood. She didn't want the way they'd always been to change when all this was over, but sometimes you couldn't stop change no matter how hard you tried. So she was going to savour every last moment of being the Gabe and Georgia they'd always been, before she finally went down for her op, because one way or another, everything *was* about to change.

'I think you should do something more exciting for me to wake up to. Maybe ask if they can do you some extensions and go for a Hulk Hogan look! He used to be your favourite when we were kids, do you remember? You even had the action figure!'

'I love you Georgia Ritchie but, even for you, I draw the line at a blond mullet.'

'A girl can dream.' The words caught in her throat as the door to her hospital room was pushed open.

'We're ready for you now.' The nurse standing in the doorway had a sing-song voice, which made it sound as if Georgia's table in her favourite restaurant was ready. This was it, the last time she'd see Gabe and be the same person she'd been when he'd asked her to marry him. She was no more ready to say goodbye than she'd thought she'd be and suddenly she wanted to cling to him and beg them not to take her away. But it was too late now. Squeezing Gabe's hand again, she nodded. She had to be strong for her husband and her mother, and whatever happened next, she'd always be grateful she'd had them in her life.

* * *

Georgia was sure she could hear Ruby barking, but she couldn't seem to open her eyes, never mind lift her head off the pillow.

'I got this on video last week, after I finally taught her how to catch the ball and bring it back without falling over when she spins around to run back to me. She was so excited she wouldn't stop barking. Poor little thing, I never realised how much only having one eye would affect her.' Gabe's voice sounded strained, but when she tried to answer him and tell him he'd already shown her the video, nothing came out.

'Oh bless her. She's such a sweet little thing.' Her mother sounded emotional too. Surely they weren't that upset just because Ruby had struggled to learn to catch a ball? She might be the clumsiest dog in the world, but her quirks were all part of her character. Georgia tried to reach out for the little dog, who was never far from her side, but her arms wouldn't seem to do as she told them to.

'When do you think she's going to wake up? I thought she'd open her eyes as soon as she heard Ruby on the video.' As Gabe spoke, Georgia tried to open her eyes again. She still couldn't do it, but at least now she remembered where she was.

'She's just sleeping a lot because of the morphine. But you heard them, they said she was fine when they brought her round after the op, otherwise they wouldn't have let us see her.'

'I suppose what they said makes sense, dosing her up on morphine for the pain and giving her body a chance to rest. I can't believe they're not watching her the whole time, though.' Gabe sighed. 'I know she's hooked up to all these machines, but what if something happens and the transplant starts to fail?'

'They watched her for the first few hours in ICU and a nurse would be here in an instant if she needed one. Try not to worry so much.' Caroline was an old hand at this, but Georgia wasn't used to her mother being the voice of reason when it came to her health. If she could have formed some words and actually made them come out of her mouth, she'd have teased her mum about suddenly becoming the calm and reasonable one. As it was, all she could do was listen.

'It's been nearly twenty-four hours now; I just didn't expect her to still be this wiped out. I can't help worrying that there's something wrong.'

'She's come through the op and both organs are working okay, that was the hardest part. We've just got to give it time.'

'I'm okay!' Georgia was shouting the words inside her head, but there was still nothing coming out.

'It's so hard trying to get my head around everything she's

been through and even she didn't expect this to happen.' Gabe's voice had taken on a much softer tone. 'I promised I wouldn't tell you, but I don't think it matters any more. We overheard you telling the nurse what Mr Kennedy said about the likelihood of finding a donor for the pancreas in time. We were both convinced there wouldn't be a transplant and so we had to do everything we could to make this summer count.'

'Oh God, I wish she'd told me.' Caroline's voice cracked. 'And that's why you decided to get married, out of the blue?'

'It felt like the right thing to do. I couldn't bear the thought of her going before we had the chance.' There was a scraping noise as someone pushed their chair back against the polished surface of the floor and Gabe's voice sounded more distant when he spoke again. 'I'm going to get a bit of air and call Ellie to let her know what's going on. Do you want me to get you anything?'

'No thank you, sweetheart. I'll wait here until you get back and then I'll pop out and call Richard; he's worried sick about her too.'

'I wish she knew how much people love her, but she always brushes that sort of stuff off.' Gabe sighed again. 'I won't be long, Caz, but call me if she wakes up, okay?'

'I will. You'll be the first person she wants to see.'

Georgia tried shaking her head as her mother spoke, but if Caroline saw it she didn't react. She didn't want to see Gabe, because when she did she'd have to tell him what she'd heard and then she'd have to face the truth. He'd only married her because he'd been convinced she was going to die. She'd always suspected the truth, but now that she knew it for sure, it was a hundred times worse than she could have imagined. It felt as though there were tears rolling down her cheeks, but she wasn't sure they really were until her mother wiped one away.

'Nurse, nurse! I think she's waking up again.' Caroline's face was fuzzy as Georgia finally managed to open her eyes. She was awake at last, but all she wanted was to go back to before she'd heard Gabe admit the truth.

* * *

'Hi Gabe. How's she doing?' Ellie snatched the phone up on the second ring, holding her breath as she waited for him to answer.

'No change as yet. The doctors are really pleased with how the kidney and pancreas are working, but she's still not fully conscious. She was in a lot of pain overnight and they had to administer some quite high doses of morphine to manage that, so they said it's to be expected. They don't seem too worried, but I just wish she'd wake up and talk to me.'

'She will soon, and it's great news that the transplant seems to have gone so well.' Ellie hadn't been able to sleep the night after the operation and, scrolling through her phone at 3 a.m., a message had popped up from her mum to ask if she was awake. She'd ended up sneaking downstairs and calling Karen for a chat, so they could try and reassure one another that everything would be okay. If it had been as bad as that for them, she couldn't even imagine how Gabe and Caroline had coped with the overnight wait whilst Georgia was monitored to see if the operation had been a success.

'There are so many things I want to tell her and so many things I want to plan for, once she's fully recovered, but I don't want to freak her out.' Gabe sounded exhausted and Ellie doubted he'd managed any sleep at all. 'All of this is going to be new to her and she's going to have a lot more options than she had before. I'm not even sure if I'll feature in her plans.'

'Sorry Gabe, I know you're probably horribly sleep deprived, but you're talking rubbish!' Ellie looked out of the kitchen window as she spoke, watching as Ben led their daughter down towards the paddocks. Mae had been full of energy all morning and she'd been desperate to go outside, but Ellie just hadn't felt up to it. Between worrying about Georgia, and the baby deciding to tap dance on her bladder, she'd barely got any sleep either. 'Georgia adores you, that's been obvious to all of us since we first met you. If this changes anything, it'll only be for the better.'

'I hope so. But when we decided to get married, I don't think she thought about it in the same way most people do. It wasn't that big of a commitment when she'd been told she probably only had until the end of the year to live. I've been in love with her since we were kids, but she never showed the slightest sign of returning those feelings until we moved to Cliffview.'

'You never told her how you felt before you lived together either though, did you?'

'No.' Gabe cleared his throat. 'But like I told you before, it was because I was scared of losing her friendship if she didn't feel the same.'

'I think that's exactly why she didn't tell you how she felt. It took her prognosis to force you both to be honest, because you knew time was running out. Except the brilliant thing is that now it isn't.'

'I'm not going to put any pressure on her; whatever she wants now is fine by me. She's waited long enough to be able to choose the life she really wants and I made a promise that, if she got through the operation okay, I'd never ask for anything again.'

'Just tell her that; it sums up exactly how you feel about

her.' Ellie held her phone in one hand, and the other hand automatically moved to her stomach as the baby decided to perform what felt like a somersault. 'Tell her that Ruby's missing her too, although she's done a pretty good job of commandeering Ginger's bed, which she seems to find much more appealing than her own!'

'Thanks for looking after Ruby and for everything else you've done.'

'It's our pleasure and, even though you won't be at Cliffview any more, we feel like we've made some friends for life.'

'You definitely have and you won't be able to get rid of us now, unless Georgia really does decide to dump me the moment she comes round!' Gabe laughed, sounding much less strained than he had a few minutes before.

'It'll be fine, Gabe, I promise. She loves you and nothing's going to change that.' Ellie wasn't in the habit of making promises she couldn't keep, but she'd have staked everything she owned on being right. But sometimes, even a sure thing turned out not to be.

15

'Are you okay?'

Georgia had her back to Gabe as he asked the question. The feeling of dread that had settled in her chest wasn't just because it felt as though she'd been asked that question 6,000 times since her transplant, but because she was finally going to have to answer it honestly. He'd never have accepted it if she'd broached the subject of ending their marriage whilst she'd been in hospital. Instead she'd replayed the words she'd overheard, when she'd still been dosed up on morphine and unable to talk, over and over, on a continuous loop inside her head. There was no getting away from it; the wedding had only gone ahead because they'd both thought she'd be dead before their first anniversary came around. Unfortunately, not even the morphine could numb the pain of realising that the person you loved more than anyone would never feel the same. She had to set him free for both of their sakes.

He'd been amazing since the operation, the same way he'd always been. Gabe was the most caring man she'd ever met, which had made her mission to fall out of love with him impossible. She'd get over him eventually, though, she had to. Or she wouldn't, but she could live with that too. The thought that she might lose his friendship as a consequence was what scared her most, and it was much worse than any pain she'd felt as a result of the operation. But she'd got through everything else and she'd have to get through this.

'This isn't working.'

'Which app is it? If you don't run any of the updates, none of them will work properly.'

'I'm not talking about my phone. I'm talking about us.' She still couldn't bring herself to turn and look at him, keeping her focus on Ruby who was rolling around on her back in the garden of Caroline's house, whilst Barney kept well out of the way. The old dog seemed relatively unfazed by Ruby's arrival, but when it all got too much he was a dab hand at hiding behind a bush, or in the gap between the garden shed and the fence. If Ruby was missing Cliffview a hundredth as much as Georgia was, then she was doing a far better job of hiding it. Between leaving Seabreeze Farm and facing up to the reality that she'd have to say goodbye to Gabe, Georgia was probably the unhappiest she'd ever been. It was much worse than when Mr Kennedy had delivered his prognosis. There'd been nothing she could do about that – no decisions she had to make – which made this so much harder.

'What do you mean?' Gabe moved next to her and she was forced to look at him, his eyes round with concern. 'I know it's not ideal us moving in with your mum until we can sort out our own place, but she's at Richard's a lot of the time anyway and I thought we were managing okay.'

'It's got nothing to do with where we're living.' Georgia had to keep her voice steady. If it cracked, even a little bit, then Gabe would know she didn't really believe what she was saying and he'd try and talk her round. He'd give up his dreams for her, she already knew that, but she couldn't let him. He was never going to be the one to say it was over, he was much too nice and that was why he deserved so much more than she could ever give him. 'It's because everything's changed. This – us living together and being married – was only ever meant to be a temporary thing.'

'Nothing's changed for me. I still want to be here.' He tried to reach out for her, but she snatched her hand away. If he touched her, she'd never go through with it. He was probably trying to convince himself every bit as much as he was her, because he'd do anything not to hurt her, even if that meant hurting himself.

'Well it's changed for me. We had nothing to lose when we decided to get married and it was supposed to be my last hurrah.'

'That's not how I remember it.' A muscle was going in his cheek, but his tone was still steady and she almost wished he'd raise his voice, so she could be sure he couldn't hear the hammering of her heart that was almost deafening inside her head.

'Would you have proposed if I hadn't been told I had less than a year to live?' She looked straight at him. 'Honestly.'

'I...' He shook his head. 'Okay, maybe it made things more urgent, but I'd have got around to it eventually.'

'Would you? Really? Or would whatever this has become between us have run its course and fizzled out?'

'We can't know what would have happened if things had been completely different. If we hadn't ended up living at Cliffview together, then maybe we'd never have realised how we felt.'

'There it is though. You said how we *felt*, not how we *feel*.'

'You're twisting my words now.' His tone had an edge to it at last, but she had to squash the surge of hope that came with the passion in his voice. If he really wanted to fight for what they had, he wouldn't be acting like this. His reaction was probably down to guilt more than anything else. Guilt at the relief of finally being able to admit the truth to her and to himself.

'I saw the text about the job offer.' Georgia arranged her features into what she hoped was a neutral expression, but the act was making her whole face ache. Since moving back to her mum's house, they were sharing the study space as a home office. Georgia was promoting the book and trying her best to keep up with the messages that came in on social media to say how much people loved *Gerry and the Great Goat Escape*, lots of them asking when there'd be a sequel. The trouble was, she hadn't felt like creating anything since the transplant and she hadn't even picked up a pencil to sketch, let alone paint anything. Gabe was running his freelance photographer business largely out of the study too, so they were sharing the Apple Mac where he did some of his photo editing. When she'd read the email she hadn't been snooping, he'd left his emails open. Maybe he'd wanted her to see it, even subconsciously, knowing she'd encourage him to take up the offer – and he'd feel better telling himself the decision had been hers.

'I'm not going to take the job.'

'You should. You've got to.' The email had been from an adventure holiday company based in Christ Church, New Zealand. The contract was to spend spring and summer in New Zealand, which ran from September to March, taking wildlife, action and nature photographs for their social media campaigns. Given that it was already late September, the company had asked for a decision as soon as possible. If Gabe threw this opportunity away, he might never get something as good come his way again.

It had forced her hand, which was probably a good thing, otherwise she might never have found the strength to push him away.

'There'll be other job offers. It's not the right time. I don't want to leave you.' Gabe reached out for her and this time she didn't pull away. Leaning in to him, she wanted to feel the solid reassurance of his body against hers one last time. She inhaled the scent of his familiar aftershave, trying to commit it all to memory.

'I want you to go so we can find our way back to being friends again one day.' Georgia swallowed hard as she forced herself to pull away, silently praying that she'd manage to get the next few sentences out without giving the truth away, when it felt like she was ripping her own heart out through her throat. 'If you stay, we'll end up resenting each other and then it will be too late to go back to how we were.'

'What if it's already too late?' Gabe's eyes had taken on a glassy sheen. 'I love you George and I still don't understand where this has come from. I thought we were doing okay.'

'But you can do so much better than okay. We both can. You're not going to change my mind, Gabe, so please don't make this difficult for me.' It was time to play her trump card. 'I've felt sick thinking about how to ask you to leave and I haven't been able to sleep either.'

It wasn't a lie. She'd barely slept in the two days since she'd read the email and decided it was now or never. What was the use of having the poor-little-me sickness card, if she couldn't play it when she needed to? Gabe wouldn't do anything to jeopardise her health, it was the one thing she could guarantee.

'I'm not going to leave just like that. We're married and, whatever you might think, those vows meant a hell of a lot to me.'

'And I'm not going to give up on making you see sense. You can either accept what I'm saying now or we can have the same conversation, over and over again, until you admit that I'm right.'

'If you want to keep talking about it, that's fine. But I'm not leaving.' Gabe sounded defeated, despite his words, and it took all she had not to reach out to him again. She loved him more than he'd ever know. He was her rock, her best friend and the one person who'd always been able to make her laugh no matter what, but that was exactly why she was letting him go. Gabe had earned the freedom to live his life for him. If it took a hundred difficult conversations to make him see sense, then that's what she'd do. Their whole relationship had been about putting Georgia's needs first. It was time to put Gabe first for once, even if it broke her heart.

Every season at the farm had its own beauty, but Ellie had to admit that autumn was probably her favourite. The land tapered to a point where it met the woodland that divided it from her parents' property. There were some evergreens amongst the woodland, but most of the trees were changing to russet and gold and there was a fresh new bite in the air, as the Indian summer finally started to fade away. The cooler nights were a welcome relief at this stage of her pregnancy and an evening walk with Ben was suddenly appealing again. Mae was in her new all-terrain pushchair, so Ben had suggested taking the coastal path that ran behind Cliffview and on to the grassy clifftop beyond it.

'I really should come out and pick some of these sloes to

make gin for after the baby arrives.' Ellie picked a berry off one of the bushes.

'I can't believe how quickly the weeks are going past. Do you think Mae's going to cope okay with being a big sister?' Ben navigated a rutty patch on the path, just before it forked off on the left down towards Cliffview.

'I think she'll be fine, although judging by the way she squeezes Ginger when she wants a cuddle, we might have to watch that she doesn't accidentally love the baby to death.' She laughed and their little dog, Ginger, doubled back at the sound of her name, before heading down the path towards Cliffview and starting to bark. 'It's okay girl, come back.'

'There's someone down there.' Ben turned the pushchair to follow Ginger. 'I thought Alan said there was no-one staying until next week.'

'He did.' Ellie suddenly felt uneasy. If there was someone strange lurking around, she didn't want Ben to follow them down there, especially not with Mae in her pushchair. The sleepless nights she'd had lately meant she'd got into the habit of reading her Kindle into the early hours of the morning and she'd discovered a new favourite author, Helen Phifer. Her books were a brilliant mix of crime and horror, which was great in the safety of Ellie's bedroom, but frankly terrifying when her imagination suddenly ran riot about the stranger lurking in the dusk. 'Let's just leave it and phone Alan when we get back.'

'I think it's Gabe.' Ben was already heading down the path and Ellie hoped he was right as she followed on behind him. Kelsea Bay was a really safe place as a rule, but there'd been some trouble with squatters trying to move into one of the holiday lets down by the harbour during the summer.

'Gabe!' Ellie shouted his name as they got closer, relief flooding her body as he turned around. Her imagination really had been running away with her. 'We thought you might be someone casing the joint.'

'Sorry, I didn't mean to scare you.' Gabe walked up the path to meet them. 'I just wanted to come up here one last time before I left Kent.'

'I didn't think Georgia could travel for a while?' Ellie frowned. Wherever they were going, it couldn't be for long. Georgia had made it her goal to be recovered enough to still be a bridesmaid at Freya's wedding in December.

'Georgia's not coming; she doesn't want to be with me any more.' Gabe's face was like a mask. 'I got offered a job in New Zealand and there was no way I was going to take it, but since she found out about it she's been relentless. Telling me the wedding was a mistake and she'd never have done it if she'd known it would last more than a year. It didn't matter what I said to her, or how many times we rowed about it, she wouldn't back down. The final straw was when I got a letter from a firm of solicitors, who are apparently representing her, saying she wants a divorce.'

'Oh God, Gabe. I'm so sorry, mate.' Ben clapped a hand on his shoulder.

'I can't believe she means it.' Ellie wanted to hug Gabe, but he looked as rigid as a concrete post and it was probably the last thing he wanted, if he was fighting to hold it all together.

'I didn't think she meant it at first, either. But it was all she wanted to talk about from the first time she mentioned it and, however I responded, she just twisted it and said it was proving her point. I don't know, maybe I was arrogant to think she couldn't possibly mean it. But when I got the letter, I had to accept it, especially as the situation was making her so stressed. I'd never forgive myself if it affected her health, so I've got to go.'

'You're going to New Zealand?' Ellie still couldn't believe it, even as Gabe nodded in response. 'How long for?'

'Six months.' He cleared his throat as he looked at her. 'We were so happy when we were living here. At least I thought we were, but now I don't know if Georgia ever really was. It was the happiest time of my life, though, strange as that might seem.'

'Maybe some time apart will change her mind and make her see sense?' Ellie was clutching at straws, but she couldn't get her head around the idea of Gabe and Georgia being apart forever.

'The divorce should be finalised by then, according to the solicitors.' There was a note of bitterness in Gabe's voice and Ellie wasn't sure she could blame him.

'Maybe one of us could talk to her?' She'd barely got the words out, before Gabe shook his head.

'I've done enough talking, reasoning and downright begging for all of us. Thanks so much for everything, but I think it's best if we just leave it. Georgia knows what she wants and she's made it obvious.' Gabe sighed. 'I'm heading to the airport in the morning and I don't think I'm up to seeing everyone first, but it would be great if you could say goodbye to your mum and dad for me, and pass on my thanks for everything they've done too?'

'Of course we will.' Ben patted his shoulder again. 'But don't be a stranger, will you? Let us know how you're getting on out there and come and see us when you get back.'

'Definitely and I want to hear all about the baby when he or she arrives.'

'We'll be in touch, as soon as there's some news.' Tears were burning at the back of Ellie's throat as Gabe walked away. She had no right to feel so upset, but she couldn't help it, and this time it had nothing to do with pregnancy hormones. Georgia was throwing something amazing away and there was nothing any of them could do about it.

Caroline hadn't been able to persuade Georgia to come back to Seabreeze Farm, even to visit Gerry's tearooms, since she'd left Cliffview. She'd felt guilty about continuing her regular trips to meet up with Karen and Ellie, but Caroline had needed their friendship more than ever lately. Especially now that Georgia and Gabe had split up and he'd jetted off to a job on the other side of the world. When she'd asked Gabe what had happened, he'd told her that she needed to talk to Georgia about it. But her daughter had just shrugged and said the relationship had run its course. It was an obvious lie and Georgia hadn't used the sort of moody, monosyllabic tone she'd had during that conversation since she'd been about fourteen. If she'd suddenly told Caroline that she didn't understand her and stormed off to her room, slamming the door behind her, it wouldn't have been a surprise.

'I'm still wondering if I should go ahead with all of this.' Caroline slid the envelopes across the table towards Ellie and Karen, as they sat in the empty tearoom after it had closed to the public. 'I felt daft enough having an engagement party at my age as it was, but now that Georgia and Gabe have split up it feels wrong.'

'It's not daft and I think we could all use a reason to celebrate.' Ellie gave her a half-smile. 'I take it you haven't heard anything from Gabe?'

'Nothing. He hasn't even posted on Facebook and he was always taking photos and posting them on there.'

'I still can't believe they've split up. It was obvious to

everyone at their wedding how in love they were.' Karen shook her head. 'I know it's got nothing to do with us, but I feel like knocking their heads together!'

'You and me both, but Georgia's always been proud and she's never wanted to be seen as a sympathy case. For some reason she seems to have got it into her head that Gabe would never have married her if she hadn't only been given a year to live, but it's been obvious for ages that they've both seen each other as more than friends.' Caroline had to agree with Karen. Sometimes she wanted to shake some sense into Georgia and tell her to forget her pride for once. But that same tenacity was what had kept Georgia fighting for so long and to expect her to suddenly change would have been a waste of time.

'That's the most frustrating bit.' Ellie adjusted her position in the chair, her baby bump now keeping her half an arm's length from the table. 'When Gabe rang me to update me on how Georgia was, after the operation, he was terrified of losing her. Not because of the transplant risk, but because he was worried she'd only gone through with the wedding because she wouldn't have the chance to live to regret it.'

'Maybe we should tell her that?' Karen looked hopeful, but Ellie was already shaking her head.

'I promised him I wouldn't interfere.'

'She won't listen anyway.' Caroline put her head in her hands. 'She'd see some hidden agenda in it and Gabe's as bad as she is now. When I told him I was sure she didn't mean any of it, he said it was up to her to be the one to say it. I just don't know what to do.'

'I think all we can do is hope that Georgia sees sense. It's still early days and, when she really starts to miss him, maybe she'll find a way to swallow her pride?' Even Ellie didn't sound convinced by what she was saying.

'I hope so, but I hate seeing her like this, and it feels wrong to be planning a wedding with Richard when she's so unhappy.'

'How do you think she'd react if you said you were calling it off because of her?' Karen raised her eyebrows and for the first time Caroline laughed.

'I'm not sure I'd live to tell the tale!'

'We'd better get down to deciding on a cake for the engagement party then, and booking a date in for the wedding.' Karen reached out and put her hand over Caroline's. 'Georgia's beaten the odds before and she can do it again. If she and Gabe are meant to be together, they'll find a way.'

'I really hope so.' Caroline pressed her lips into a thin line. She'd thought all her prayers had been answered when Georgia had finally been given a transplant and it had gone so well. But now she was back to living day by day and waiting for the call that could change everything for the better. A happy ending should have been much easier to hope for this time around, but knowing Georgia like she did, it seemed less likely than ever.

16

Georgia stared at the Christmas tree. Whichever way she turned it, somehow it didn't look right. If she put the side that had lain flat against the boot of the car to the front, it looked as if the world's strongest man had sat on it. If she put that side to the wall, there was a weird gap in the middle on the other side, which looked as if someone had punched a fist through it. Much longer of fiddling with it and there was likely to be a second fist-shaped hole in it, but only if she didn't just give in and chuck the whole thing out of the back door first. God knows why she'd thought that decorating a tree would put her in the mood for Christmas anyway. She hadn't been in the mood for anything other than misery since Gabe had left. And it was all her fault.

'Argh!' Georgia wrestled with the tree again, losing her temper as one of the branches pinged back and whipped her across the face. Poor Ruby was so startled, she misjudged her attempt to jump off the sofa to find somewhere to hide and ended up in a heap on the floor. 'Sorry darling.' Scooping her up, Georgia curled up on the sofa with Ruby on her lap. Barney, who was sitting in the basket by the French windows, bathed in a shaft of winter sunlight, opened his eyes and gave her what could only be described as a dirty look, before closing them again and resuming his snooze. Even the dogs had had enough of her and she couldn't blame them; she'd had enough of herself too.

Picking up her phone, she scrolled through Instagram again. There were still no posts from Gabe's personal account, but the adventure holiday company he was working for had tagged his business account into some of the latest photos. They were from an expedition to the mountains of Wakatipu Basin in Queenstown. It looked absolutely stunning and Gabe must have been loving every minute. Seeing the opportunities he'd finally had the chance to take made her feel a tiny bit better. It didn't make her miss him any less, but at least it was a reminder of why she'd done what she'd done.

It was funny, she hadn't really thought beyond actually persuading him to leave, what it would be like not to see him all the time. They'd been together their whole lives, following one another to the same nursery, schools, college and even university, which meant they'd shared a lifetime of memories before they moved into Cliffview. It had taken about four weeks before Ruby had stopped looking for Gabe everywhere and pawing at the door with ridiculous excitement every time someone rang the doorbell, only to pine again when it wasn't him. Georgia knew exactly how she felt.

Over the years they'd developed their own traditions for important events, and Christmas was the biggest of those. Even going out to pick a tree without him had felt strange and she'd ended up grabbing more or less the first one she'd seen, from the farm shop where they'd always bought their trees. No wonder she'd ended up with such a sorry specimen.

Clicking on her Facebook app, she sighed. She knew as well as anyone that Facebook was all about showing off the best side of your life, where families looked like they were enjoying every moment of their perfect pre-Christmas celebrations and couples couldn't wait to share how romantic their holiday season was turning out to be. It wasn't the place to confess that you'd cried over your choice of Christmas tree, or tell the world how guilty you felt about receiving a double transplant when you weren't doing anything to make the most of life. No-one wanted to read that, especially not at Christmas.

There were some notifications on her profile. Most of them related to Freya and Ollie's upcoming wedding, and some photos that had been added to the album from her mum and Richard's engagement party. It had been a lovely night and Ben had read out a message of congratulations sent by Gabe, to accompany the case of champagne he'd sent. It seemed he'd been in touch with everyone except her. It was no surprise, given how explosive the ending had been when he'd opened the solicitor's letter. It had been intended as a shock tactic and it had worked, leaving Georgia reeling almost as much as Gabe. She hadn't done anything to progress the divorce yet, but she'd made herself a promise to tackle it in the New Year.

The last notification on her Facebook profile was a public post that Karen had tagged her into, from the page she still ran for organ donation awareness. Clicking on the original post, she could see it was from a man who'd received a heart transplant that had saved his life and who'd written an open letter to thank the donor whose heart he'd been given.

To My Amazing Donor,
    I know you can't read this, but it might help one of your family members eventually, or the family of another donor, to

read this and understand just how big a gift you've given me.

Christmas is a time for gifts, after all, and for thanking the most important people in our lives for being there. I can't write directly to your family yet, as I've been advised not to do so before Christmas in case it adds to their pain, and I can't write to you, or send you a gift. Not that any gift in the world would be enough; the only thing I can offer is a promise to live my life to the full and try to be a worthy recipient of the incredible gift you gave me.

Before I had the transplant, I couldn't play with my children, I didn't have the energy. Just walking from my bed to the bathroom left me breathless and exhausted. This year I was able to go and watch my daughter's nativity play and see my son sing in his school's Christmas concert, just four months after I received your heart.

I haven't been able to work in years, but I've just started volunteering for a food bank, to try in some small way to begin to repay the gift you gave me. Everything I do, I'll be doing in your honour. I'll get to watch my children open their Christmas presents this year and play with them, helping them put together their Lego sets and interfere in their craft projects, like every good dad should do. I can only do that because of you, but I don't even know your name.

What I do know is that you were forty-five, a husband and a father to two teenage daughters. I can't even begin to imagine how much your family are missing you this Christmas, but if and when I finally get to meet them, and wrap my arms around them, I'll be hugging them for you.

I won't waste a moment of the time I've been given, otherwise what was the point of your heart coming to me instead of someone else? I've been lucky all my life, despite contracting a virus that damaged my heart beyond repair. I was lucky to have people in my life who loved and supported me, even when I was so far from being the man I wanted to be. Most of all I was lucky to receive the gift of your heart and I promise to do everything I can to show how much it means to me.

Yours with immeasurable gratitude,

Jack

Georgia was sobbing by the time she got to the end of the letter. The tears were for Jack, his donor and his donor's family, but most of all they were for the family of the donor whose kidney and pancreas she had received. And for Cindy, whose incredible offer she hadn't needed to accept. She'd let them down by doing the opposite of what Jack had done. Maybe that was why she hadn't felt able to write to them. What would she say? That she was sitting at home every day, watching *This Morning* and *Loose Women*, and making excuses about why she couldn't meet up with friends, or start a new art project, let alone think about producing the artwork for a sequel to *Gerry and the Great Goat Escape*.

She'd lectured Gabe about not wasting the opportunities he'd been given. But what was the point of going through the almost unbearable pain of losing him, if she didn't follow her own advice? Whether Karen had meant it as a wake-up call when she'd tagged Georgia into that post, or whether it had far less meaning, it had achieved what nothing else had managed to do since Gabe had left, and given her a huge kick up the proverbial. She owed it to her donor to give something back and the first thing she was going to do was contact Karen, and Steve at One Wish, to see if she could help with donor aware-ness or any upcoming One Wish campaigns. Doing something positive might be the first step to getting over losing Gabe, because sitting around and feeling sorry for herself certainly hadn't worked. Either way, there was nothing left to lose.

* * *

Steve from One Wish was coming across the dance floor towards Georgia, swaying his hips from side to side and doing the sort of dad-style dancing that would make any child over the age of ten want to hide under the table. It was making Georgia laugh, though, which was no doubt his intention.

'Come on then, are you going to give me my promised dance?' He was still clicking his fingers, but his arms were now raised above his head, as he continued to shake his bum like a wannabe carnival dancer who didn't quite have what it took.

'I don't mind dancing with you, but not like that!' She grinned as he did another twirl.

'What's the matter? Worried you can't keep up with me?'

'Absolutely.'

'Oh hold on.' He paused as the band finished their rendition of 'Despacito'. 'You might be lucky, if they change the pace.'

'You do know there are two types of luck don't you? Good luck and back luck.' She couldn't help laughing as the music changed and the band broke into 'Careless Whisper'. Clearly someone was determined she should dance with Steve and she had no excuse now. 'Come on then, let's have a shuffle round. We might as well get it over and done with.'

'You'll be begging me for a second dance in a minute.' Steve took her hand and led her to the middle of the dance floor, where Freya and Ollie had been cheered on during their first dance less than an hour before. 'And, for your information, I don't do shuffling around anywhere, let alone the dance floor. Just because I'm in my fifties now, it doesn't mean I haven't still got it.' He was laughing as he twirled her around and dipped her back, making her feel like the just-for-comedy contestant they always seemed to have on *Strictly*. Steve might have twenty-five years on her, but she really was going to struggle to keep up. It would probably have been easier for him to man handle a fridge around his kitchen.

'I'm not sure if I've got it in me to cope with a second dance.'

'Are you okay?' For once Steve sounded serious, looking down at her as she tried to follow his steps and not trip over her own feet. 'You seem to be holding up brilliantly with the demands of bridesmaid duties, but it must have been a long day and it's only been three months since your transplants.'

'It's been lovely, but I think I'll be out for the count as soon as my head hits the pillow tonight. Thankfully, I haven't left any of my shopping until the last minute Christmas Eve dash.'

'Damn. I knew I'd forgotten to do something.' Steve laughed again. 'What have you got planned for Christmas Day?'

'I'll be with Mum and Richard, although I do feel like a bit of gooseberry hanging out with a newly engaged couple.' Georgia blinked, trying to wipe out the mental image of Gabe that had popped into her head; all the Christmases they'd shared and how he'd always tried to make them special or cheer her up when she'd been feeling down. The time when he'd come into her hospital ward dressed as Christmas cracker was a particular highlight. But this would be the first Christmas in her entire life when Gabe wouldn't have any part in the celebrations.

'I'm sure your mum and Richard don't feel that way. Have you told her about our plans yet?'

'She thinks it's a great idea and I can't wait to get started.' Georgia felt a warm glow of excitement just talking about the prospect of starting to paint again. Finally having something to look forward to was the only thing that was getting her through a Christmas without her best friend. When she'd approached Steve to see if she could do something else for One Wish, they'd brainstormed a few ideas. She couldn't even contemplate starting a sequel to *Gerry and the Great Goat Escape* without Gabe, but there were lots of other things she could do.

In the end they'd agreed that she would concentrate on developing enough pieces for an art exhibition to raise funds and awareness for One Wish. The plan was for her to turn some of the wishes the charity had granted into paintings, using the photographs that had been taken of the events, some of which had been photographed by Gabe. When Steve had started to pick out the pictures he thought would work best, more than half of them had been Gabe's work and she'd recognised it without having to be told they were his. It had been bittersweet going through them. It made her miss him more than ever, but it also made it feel like they were still linked in a way that could never really be broken.

'What about you? What are you doing for Christmas?' Georgia could see Ellie rubbing her back as she stood on the opposite side of the room. The baby was due in less than a week's time, but no-one would have guessed it from the way Ellie had run around all day. She still looked great, despite her fears that she'd be like an elephant in a tutu by the time the wedding came around.

'We're at home. Both the kids and their partners are coming to stay over from tomorrow until New Year's Eve. My son's girl-friend doesn't know it yet, but he's planning to propose on

Christmas morning. I just hope she says yes, or it could be very awkward!'

'Oh my God, it really could!'

'Talking of which...' Steve released her from his grip. 'I think this is probably a good time for me to excuse myself, before being a third wheel has the potential to get very awkward indeed.'

'What are you talking about?' Georgia turned to follow Steve's gaze and all the air felt as if it had been sucked out of her lungs in one big whoosh. Gabe was walking across the dance floor towards her and she had to screw up and open her eyes twice over, before she could believe it was really him.

'Hello George.' He smiled, but she seemed to have forgotten how to breathe, let alone talk. 'I've missed you.'

'Umm.' It came out as a weird, strangled sort of sound and all she could do was nod. She'd missed him more than she'd ever thought possible, and she wasn't sure she'd ever find the words to express just how much. Now Gabe was home, but she had no idea why or how long he'd stay.

17

Georgia was awake, but she was scared to open her eyes in case Gabe wasn't there when she did. She didn't have a good enough imagination to wonder if his arrival at Freya and Ollie's wedding was a dream, but she was terrified he might have disappeared as quickly as he'd arrived. He'd come back to her mum's place with her after the wedding, as Caroline was staying at Richard's. They'd talked late into the evening about everything and, for the first time ever, she'd been completely honest about how she felt. She'd told him about overhearing the conversation in the hospital, eventually realising she'd misinterpreted it because of her own insecurities.

For his part, Gabe had confessed that he'd only left and broken off all contact in a last ditch attempt to make her realise they were meant to be together. It had worked. And when he'd walked across the dance floor towards her, all her doubts had disappeared. But she couldn't speak for Gabe; he might not have had that same overwhelming feeling of love when he saw her. He could have woken up in the night, with nagging doubts about whether coming home had been the right thing to do after all, and jumped straight on the next plane back to New Zealand.

'Morning.' He was watching her when she finally opened her eyes, with a huge grin on his face that she couldn't help mirroring.

'Morning.' Reaching out her hand, she intertwined it with his. 'I was worried you might have decided to go back home in the night.'

'I am home.' He caressed the palm of her hand with his fingertips, making her skin tingle. 'And I'm not going anywhere until the New Year. I don't want to go back at all, but I've got to finish the contract if I don't want to blow my professional reputation for good.'

'I wish you didn't have to go back either, but I've got to admit having you home is a pretty good Christmas present.'

'Pretty good?' He grinned again, pulling her towards him. 'I think we can do better than that.'

* * *

'Was everything okay with your mum?' Gabe called over from where he was standing by the oven, cooking them both a late breakfast.

'She's fine. She was just phoning to tell me that Ellie gave birth to a little boy at seven o'clock this morning.' Georgia grabbed some cutlery out of the drawer to set the table. 'How amazing is that? Holding on for the wedding reception and then heading straight to the hospital to give birth? She'll be back home by this afternoon.'

'That's brilliant and they're both doing okay?'

'Really well. They haven't decided on a name yet, but

Karen's going to send some photos through to Mum and she'll forward them on to us. I can't wait to meet him!'

'Neither can I.' Gabe tipped scrambled eggs on to the toast and brought the plates over to the table. 'I'm looking forward to seeing Ellie and Ben again too. The last time I saw them I was virtually crying on their shoulders, the day before I left for New Zealand.'

'They've been so great since you left, getting in touch to check I was okay and trying to encourage me to go up to the farm, but I just couldn't face it without you there. Going up there for the wedding yesterday was the first time I've done it since we left Cliffview.'

'I owe Ben and Ellie a debt too. They both rang me separately when I was in New Zealand, to tell me why they thought you'd asked me to leave, even though you didn't really want me to.'

'Did they? Funnily enough, Ellie told me something you'd said to her after my operation. It was partly what made me realise how stupid I was being trying to push you away, just to protect myself. If you hadn't come home, I was going to try and call you on Christmas Day and tell you I'd made the biggest mistake of my life.'

'Now that would have shocked me! You've always been so determined not to show even the tiniest chink in your armour.'

'I decided I didn't have anything left to lose. I'd already lost you once and nothing could be worse than that.'

'I like this new vulnerable you.' Gabe laughed as she pulled a face. 'Don't worry, I won't get too used to it. If it hadn't worked out so well, I'd have a bone to pick with Ellie and Ben; they promised not to interfere.'

'Me too, but thank God they did.'

'They weren't the only ones.' Gabe looked across at her.

'Your mum rang me, so did Karen, and even Steve from One Wish!'

'Oh my God, really?' Even as she asked the question, Georgia knew he was telling the truth. But she couldn't pretend to be annoyed, not when it had brought Gabe home.

'Uh huh. They say it takes a village to raise a child, but it looks like it took a good chunk of Kelsea Bay to get us back together.'

'I think I can forgive them.' Leaning across the table, she planted a kiss on his lips, silently offering up a thank you for having so many people in their lives who cared enough to try and fix things.

'Me too.' Gabe nodded, as she sat back into her seat. 'But you need to finish your breakfast before it's stone cold, and we've got to go out afterwards and get your present.'

'Oh no. Please don't give me a present, I haven't got you anything and I feel awful.'

'You can make it up to me later.' Gabe grinned again and she wouldn't argue with that. She'd spend every day making up for her mistake, but in a weird kind of way she was glad they'd gone through it. Otherwise she might never have realised just how lucky she was to have him and there was no way she'd make the same mistake twice.

* * *

Ruby was so close to Gabe that if he'd stepped back he'd definitely have trodden on her. Ever since they'd picked her up from Richard's house, where she and Barney had been looked after by his sons during the wedding, she'd refused to leave his side. She was almost as delighted as Georgia to have him home.

Richard had invited Gabe to the planned Christmas celebrations at his house the next day, along with Georgia, Caroline and his two sons, Jamie and Dan. Georgia had got to know her stepbrothers-to-be a bit more since her mum and Richard had got engaged. They were lovely boys who already seemed really fond of Caroline and the next year promised to be filled with reasons to celebrate. All of her check-ups so far had gone well too and the one thing she was trying not to think about was the prospect of Gabe going away again. She could just about cope with the knowledge that he had to complete his contract in New Zealand, but it was what came after that which really worried her. The whole point of going to New Zealand had been to drive his career forward and he couldn't let that momentum come to nothing. It was Christmas Eve though and she wasn't going to think about that, at least not for today.

'Where are we going?' Gabe had driven them along the coast road to Kelsea Bay and pulled up in the small car park between the harbour and the delicatessen that Ben's mother and sister ran between them. They'd managed to get the only space and there were quite a few people in town, doing some last minute shopping. It was the sort of cool, crisp and sunny day that made it feel amazing to be alive. If she managed to sneak off at some point, maybe she'd get the chance to buy Gabe a present from one of the gift shops. After all, who didn't want to unwrap a carved driftwood heart, or a sweatshirt featuring a picture of the Kelsea Bay lighthouse, on Christmas morning?

'Like I said, it's your Christmas present. Just a couple more minutes and you'll find out.' Gabe took her hand, leading her under the archway that led to the far side of the harbour, where a row of fisherman's cottages were nestled into a carved out hollow below the cliff, set just far enough forward to let the light flood in.

'Is it one of those sculptures they sell in *Driftwood Island*?' Georgia suddenly didn't feel so bad about her choice of last minute gifts, but Gabe shook his head.

'No, it's this.' Stopping outside the last cottage, he bent down towards the front step and pulled a key out from underneath a rock to the right-hand side of the door. 'Happy Christmas, George.'

'I don't understand.' Her mind was working overtime, trying to process what was going on, but the conclusions it was coming up with didn't make any sense. There was no way the key could be for the cottage and, even it was, there was no chance it belonged to them.

'I arranged the mortgage on the cottage when you when you were in the hospital, using the money Nan left me as a deposit. I wanted it to be a surprise when you were well enough to think about moving out of your mum's, only we never got that far. Last summer was the best time of my life and, even though this might not quite be able to compete with Cliffview, it's got views of the Channel out of every window at the front, and a back garden just big enough to keep Ruby entertained. I wanted our first home to be in Kelsea Bay and, when this came up for sale, it felt like it was meant to be.'

'Oh Gabe, it's amazing.' Throwing her arms around his neck, she hesitated. 'But what about your work? Being tucked away in Kelsea Bay might be my dream, but it isn't yours.'

'I've agreed to go back to New Zealand and work seven days a week, so I can finish my contract in six weeks, but after that I'll be starting a new job.'

'Not at the photographers in the high street?' Georgia's heart sank. She couldn't let him sacrifice everything for her, not even now.

'No, I'll be working for a photographic agency that supplies pictures for hundreds of magazines, including *BBC Wildlife*. I sent them some pictures I took during my free time in New Zealand and they loved them.' Gabe put his arms around her waist, pulling her closer to him. 'And the publishers want us to write another book, as well as the sequel to *Gerry and the Great Goat Escape*. I had some ideas for another story when I was in New Zealand and I've got the photographs that gave me the idea, so I just need an artist who can bring them to life.'

'Have you got someone in mind?' She smiled as he furrowed his brow, pretending to think about it.

'Well there is someone who produced the artwork for a masterpiece called Peabody and the Coconuts. I'm hoping she might be interested in a joint venture.'

'Oh, I think you can guarantee she'll be interested in whatever joint ventures you want to suggest from now on.' Laughing as he scooped her into his arms and carried her over the threshold into their new house, she couldn't help thinking that maybe a driftwood heart would make the perfect addition to their new home after all. She could never compete with the gifts she'd been given since the start of the summer, because life, love and friendship were priceless. So a driftwood heart would just have to do.

ACKNOWLEDGMENTS

I have to start the acknowledgements with a huge thank you to all the readers who have chosen to read the *Seabreeze Farm* series and for the many lovely reviews the books have received so far. I hope you've enjoyed this third novel in the series. Sadly, I don't own a donkey sanctuary, but I was born a stone's throw from the cliffs that overlook the English Channel. I also grew up on a small holding, where taking in stray animals was a fairly regular event and, by the time I'd left home, I'd done everything from covering the night shift feeds for abandoned lambs to delivering a foal with nothing more than the aid of an *Encyclopaedia Britannica* – long before the days of Google! So I've drawn upon a lot of personal experiences to write the Seabreeze Farm series and it's very close to my heart as a result.

This book is dedicated to my inspirational cousin, Kathy. Like Georgia, the protagonist, Kathy has faced far more than her fair share of health challenges, but she's built an amazing new life for herself and has been truly inspirational in the personal transformation she's undergone.

The support for my books from bloggers and reviewers continues to be incredible and I can't thank them enough. To all the readers who also take the time to get in touch, it means such a lot to me and I feel so privileged to be doing the job I spent my whole childhood dreaming of.

If you haven't already signed up to my newsletter you can find the link on my Twitter account and Facebook Author page.

There are lots of opportunities to enter competitions and contribute to the books by naming a character or, in the case of the Seabreeze Farm series, an animal! You'll also receive exclusive free short stories from time to time too. The Seabreeze Farm series will be continuing beyond this book, but it will be taking a slightly different direction and focusing on the veterinary practice that Ben runs, which is set to move to a converted building on the farm. This new location will give lots of scope for more mischievous animals to take centre stage and I look forward to sharing the stories with you.

My thanks as always go to the team at Boldwood Books for their help, especially my amazing editor, Emily Ruston, for lending me her wisdom to get this book into the best possible shape and set the scene for the next book in the series. Thanks too to my wonderful copy editor and proofreader, Candida, for all her hard work. I'm really grateful to Nia, Claire and the rest of the team for all their work behind the scenes and especially for marketing the books so brilliantly, and to Amanda for having the vision to set up such a wonderful publisher to work with.

As ever, I can't sign off without thanking my writing tribe, The Write Romantics, and all the other authors who I am lucky enough to call friends.

Finally, as they always will, my biggest thank you goes to my family for their support, patience, love and belief in the years it took to get to this point. I love you all more than you'll ever know.

MORE FROM JO BARTLETT

We hope you enjoyed reading *One Last Summer at Seabreeze Farm*. If you did, please leave a review.

If you'd like to gift a copy, this book is also available as an ebook, hardback, large print, digital audio download and audiobook CD.

Sign up to Jo Bartlett's mailing list for news, competitions and updates on future books.

http://bit.ly/JoBartlettNewsletter

Why not explore the top 10 bestselling The Cornish Midwives series:

ABOUT THE AUTHOR

Jo Bartlett is the bestselling author of over nineteen women's fiction titles. She fits her writing in between her two day jobs as an educational consultant and university lecturer and lives with her family and three dogs on the Kent coast.

 twitter.com/J_B_Writer

 facebook.com/JoBartlettAuthor

 instagram.com/jo_bartlett123

Boldw**oo**d

Boldwood Books is an award-winning fiction publishing company seeking out the best stories from around the world.

Find out more at www.boldwoodbooks.com

Join our reader community for brilliant books, competitions and offers!

Follow us
@BoldwoodBooks
@BookandTonic

Sign up to our weekly deals newsletter

https://bit.ly/BoldwoodBNewsletter

Printed in Great Britain
by Amazon

20912749R00129